EDDIE

by

C.C. Parfoot

A catalogue record for this book is available from the National Library of Australia

ISBN: 978-0-6456448-0-7 (ebook)
ISBN: 978-0-6456448-1-4 (paperback)

Cover art and design by Laura Burgin and Roger Burgin

First ebook and paperback edition December 2022

This book is for Lyndal, Ethan, Isaac, and Jared

with love from Dad.

Chapter 1

One warm November afternoon, not long after school and well before dinner, William Craft, Crafty to his friends, was tinkering with his latest project.

He was sitting on a tall stool at his father's work bench in the back shed. On the bench in front of him was a polished metal cylinder. This wasn't any ordinary metal cylinder. This one had arms and legs and a hemispherical head with micro-dot-cameras for eyes and a small slot for a mouth, behind which was a super-minitiaurised sound bar.

A hatch was open at the side and Crafty was poking around inside with a tiny screwdriver. In his other hand was a soldering iron and every now and again he would touch its slender, super-hot tip to one of the miniature circuit boards. A thin trail of white smoke drifted out and up and dissolved somewhere beyond the boy's left shoulder, leaving its acrid smell in the air.

Crafty carefully placed the soldering iron back in its cradle and began tapping the handle of the screwdriver thoughtfully against his chin.

"Well," he said, letting out a satisfied breath. "That's about it." What he saw pleased him. "Not bad for a prototype."

The metal cylinder with arms and legs and a hemispherical head with micro-dot-cameras for eyes and super-miniaturised sound bar for a mouth lay absolutely still, almost as if it were expecting some final touch.

Crafty rummaged around in a drawer until his fingers found the blister pack he'd opened and put there earlier in the day. With great ceremony, he took two shiny silver AAA batteries from what was left in the jumbo-sized packet.

"Drum roll please," he said in his most serious voice to no one in particular, enjoying the drama of the occasion. "The moment has arrived. Here, in this shed, in this otherwise unremarkable suburban backyard, we are about to make history!"

Carefully, Crafty fiddled the batteries through the gap so they fit into the space open at the side of the cylinder. He pressed them into place, and gently closed the flap until it clicked. He took a deep breath and pushed the little black switch at the base of the cylinder to 'On.'

Nothing happened.

"Oh, great," Crafty groaned. He felt his heart sink with disappointment.

He went through all the schematics in his head, trying to figure out what had gone wrong.

What had he missed? What was wrong with his design?

In the quiet of the shed, he could hear a noise. A noise that hadn't been there before. It was the sound of a tiny fan spinning up to full speed. He looked down at the cylinder with arms and legs and noticed that the micro-dot-camera eyes had started to glow a soft and restful green.

"Of course!" Crafty exclaimed. "Valves! They take time to warm up. I should have remembered that."

"Always use valves for reliability," his grandfather had told him. *"Valves will last hundreds of years. More if you look after them. Some of Edison's inventions still work. And he used valves."* So Crafty had too.

The micro-dot-cameras slowly brightened and then a very small and very electronic voice said: "Hello."

The little machine sounded the word out slowly and deliberately, as if the shape of it was unfamiliar.

There was a blip; the clearing of a brand new unused electronic throat. "Hello."

Crafty sat back on the stool. He had expected a bit more than just "hello," but it was a good start. *"Early days,"* he said to himself. *"This little guy has a long way to go and a lot to learn."*

There was another blip, this one slightly longer. "Should I have said good morning, or is it more correct to say good afternoon? My internal clock is wrong. I'm sure it's not midnight. Hello will be acceptable in that case, won't it?"

"It works," Crafty shouted. "It really, really works!" He was almost jumping around the shed in his excitement.

"Yes," said the very small and very electronic voice. "It seems that way, doesn't it?" The little machine swivelled its head to look directly at Crafty. "Didn't you think it was going to?"

It appeared to Crafty as if the micro-dot-cameras twinkled, which of course was impossible.

"Although," that little voice said.

"Yes? Although... What do you mean? Although?"

"There is something...," said the little electronic voice.

"What ...?" Crafty asked, picking up on the urgency in the little machine's tone.

"Not quite right."

"What?" Crafty knew he was sounding dumb and not coming across at all like the genius inventor that he was. The more Crafty thought about it, the less able he was to put his finger on what the problem might be.

"I am not able to move," said the little machine, matter-of-factly.

Crafty frowned. "That's not right. You should be able to. You have the very best quality servo motors that pocket money can buy. You should be jumping around!"

The little micro-dot-cameras pulsed. There was a strained whirring as if the little machine was trying to stand up. But nothing happened.

"I am sorry, I must confirm, I am unable to move."

"Have you run your diagnostics?" Crafty asked hopefully.

"What are ... Di...ag...nos...tics?"

"They are computer programs that check your system and tell you what's not working properly."

"... Um, yes," said the electronic voice. "I seemed to know that already."

"Of course, it's all in your data set," Crafty declared proudly. "And if you don't have it, we can install it! Of course, we would have to recognise what is missing to begin with. That's the hardest part."

"Yes. I seem to know lots of things already."

"And?"

"And?"

"Are you planning to share?"

"Share?"

"When you find out something, when you discover a new piece of information you are designed to share. That's why I made you. To help me solve problems and stuff."

"Oh. And what would I be sharing again?" The little electronic voice sounded confused.

"The results of the diagnostics?"

"Oh. Yes. I do beg your pardon," the little machine said. "I forgot. They were running in the background. Um, let's see. Systems check as nominal, except, there isn't enough power to my servo motors. Or to anything else really. Even speaking is a strain."

"I wonder what's causing that," Crafty mused. "Maybe a wiring fault? Perhaps I have routed the power to the wrong place? A dry solder joint? A faulty diode?" Although he couldn't think where it might be, any short circuit should have been obvious to him, it would give off sparks, puffing out clouds of smelly ozone.

"Batteries," declared the little electronic voice.

"Batteries?"

"The batteries you have given me ... They are inadequate for the task." The small but now weak electronic voice drained away to silence.

And with that, the happy little glow faded from his green micro-dot-camera eyes.

Chapter 2

S uddenly there was a loud knocking on the shed door.

"Oh no," breathed Crafty, fearing the worst.

"William?" said a loud voice, that matched the loud knocking, the sound waves splitting through the wood like an axe.

"Yes Mum?"

"What happened to the batteries that were in the bottom drawer? I need some for the TV remote!"

Crafty's thoughts came in a flurry: "*Oh great! Really? Why now? What for? She never watches television.*"

"Erm ... you mean the triple A's?" For a moment he thought he might be able to fool her into thinking he'd used them all, but that wouldn't be honest, and he knew he'd feel bad about it afterwards, and besides she'd know. She had that radar they installed in mother's that detected fibs, and it was as finely tuned as it would go, it was stretched so tight, it positively twanged.

"Um, yeah, I've got them," he called. He took a big handful from the packet and slipped them into his pocket, so he had plenty for later, then he opened the shed door a crack to prevent his mother from seeing what was on the workbench. He wasn't ready to reveal his invention to the world just yet.

"Another project? Honestly." His mother said, holding out her hand.

Crafty gave her what was left of the battery pack and plied her with his most disarming grin. Sometimes it worked, and sometimes it didn't.

"Honestly," she said again, exasperated. "I don't know what you do with them."

"Sorry Mum," Crafty said.

"All right. I'll add them to the shopping list. But you might have to do extra chores to work off your debt! Or maybe we can pay you your allowance in batteries instead?" She raised an eyebrow and smiled. Crafty groaned. He hoped she wasn't serious. With Mum you could never tell.

"I'll be starting dinner soon," she told him.

"Thanks Mum, I am kind of hungry."

"You make sure you come when I call."

"Yes Mum."

"And you have homework to do!"

"Yes Mum."

"And music practice!"

"Yes Mum."

"And don't leave it all to the last minute!"

"Yes Mum," Crafty replied automatically. "I mean no, Mum, I'll get it done."

Crafty closed the door and returned to his place at the work bench. He popped the old batteries out and put new ones in and slowly the micro-dot-cameras began to glow again.

"Can you isolate your servo motors? Just the servo motors." Crafty asked when he was sure that everything was working again. "We need to conserve battery power until I can work out how to boost output."

"If I isolate power as you have suggested," the little machine said, "Then it is feasible to extend battery life to… just under an hour."

"An hour? Oh, great," Crafty checked his watch. "That brings us almost to homework time, and with the couple of sets of batteries we have left," he patted his pocket, "we have a little under two hours to find a solution!"

"And that's if Mum is slow getting dinner ready! Hopefully she gets side-tracked, which she often does," Crafty thought, but he didn't say it out loud.

"The power reserves will last longer, William, if you switch me off," the little machine said helpfully.

"Switch you off?" Crafty exclaimed. "Why would I want to do that? I just got you running. You're alive now, and learning, and I don't want to compromise that. Besides, two heads are better than one. You can help me work this out!"

"Me?" the little voice squeaked.

"Yes, you," Crafty said. "One reason I made you is to help solve problems, just like this one. To work out what's wrong, and how to fix it. Sometimes that's easier said than done."

The little machine looked dubious if that were possible. "Then I am a *computer*?"

"Yes. A supercomputer. Of sorts. And you are at the cutting edge of AI."

"Excuse me, William?"

"Yes?"

"What am I called?"

"Called?" Crafty said in a distracted tone, his mind on the power problem.

"Yes. Do I have a name?"

"Hmmm ... Of course you do."

The little machine waited expectantly; its green micro-dot-camera eyes glowing.

"What is it?"

"EDDIE."

"EDDIE?" said the little machine. "That's a strange name to give a supercomputer. What does it mean?"

"Electronic Data Digester and Inference Engine," said Crafty proudly. "E ... D ... D ... I ... E. But *never ever* with full stops, it's your name after all, it's *not* just an acronym."

"EDDIE," said EDDIE. "Thank you, William, I think that is an excellent name."

There was a hush in the shed as they both thought about different things.

"William," EDDIE said.

"Yes EDDIE?"

"I'm a sort of supercomputer, and my name is EDDIE?"

"Yes, EDDIE, but you are more than that. You are a robot."

"I'm a robot?" EDDIE asked. "And robots are different from supercomputers?"

"Yes, EDDIE, supercomputers stay in a room somewhere. They aren't portable, like you are. I made you so you could move around and do stuff. Be independent, you know? So I didn't have to carry you everywhere, like my laptop. And you are small enough to put you in my backpack if I have to. Not that you are heavy."

"Thank you for the clarification, William."

"Oh, and EDDIE?" said Crafty.

"Yes William?"

"Only my mother calls me William."

"Oh. I do apologise. What should I call you?"

"All my friends call me Crafty."

"Crafty?" EDDIE said, sounding uncertain.

"Not because I am sneaky or anything, it's because I am always making stuff, like I made you."

"If I am to call you Crafty that means I am your friend too? Doesn't it?"

"Yes, of course." said Crafty. "Don't ever doubt it. Now, let's get to work, we need to get to the bottom of this problem ... we need to give you more power, more consistently. For a start, I am sure you are tired of staring at the ceiling," and with that Crafty propped EDDIE up against the toolbox on the bench. "It might help if you saw the world from a different angle."

Several minutes dragged by with only the sound of EDDIE's fan and the clacking of his relays filling the quiet of the shed and Crafty tapping his teeth with a pencil while he thought.

EDDIE's eyes glowed a deep emerald green and every now and again he emitted a small electronic blip as if that somehow helped him to think.

"I think I have a solution," EDDIE said after what seemed like an eternity.

"Yes?" Crafty, who had been slouching, sat bolt upright, and leaned forward expectantly.

"How much pocket money do you have?"

Crafty did a quick mental calculation. "I've got about $7.00. That's not going to get us very far. What do you have in mind?"

"Is $7.00 enough to buy a new packet of batteries?"

Crafty raised a quizzical eyebrow.

"Well, if it is, then that just might give us enough time to come up with a more permanent solution," EDDIE explained.

"I can't keep feeding you batteries. For one thing I can't afford it. Hang on, what? … Tesla!" Crafty suddenly exclaimed; it sounded like a sneeze.

"I beg your pardon?" EDDIE asked.

"Nicola Tesla!"

"Excuse me?" If EDDIE had eyebrows, he'd have raised one, instead his left micro-dot-camera eye glowed a brighter green.

"Nicola Tesla, you know, the lightning guy?" Crafty said.

EDDIE whirred in what sounded like frustration. He had tried to find a reference to Nicola Tesla but couldn't and realised that he was new, and his programming wasn't yet complete.

"Tesla wanted to find a way to transmit electricity through the air without using wires!" Crafty explained. "The guy was an absolute genius!"

"Without wires?" EDDIE mused, trying to catch the train of Crafty's thought. "Is that possible?"

"Got to get you patched into Wi-Fi," Crafty muttered.

"How do you plan to do that?" asked EDDIE thinking about electricity without wires.

"I have to activate your modem and give you the password."

"Will that help with my power?"

"What? No. It won't. It'll give you Wi-Fi."

"Oh," said EDDIE as if he understood when he wasn't clear on Wi-Fi at all.

"What I am proposing to do is set up some kind of carrier wave, to piggyback the power we need, we can tap into that and ... whamo ...!"

"Whamo?" EDDIE didn't like that concept at all. "Are my internal workings designed for whamo, Crafty? It doesn't sound comfortable."

13

But Crafty wasn't listening. "In the early days of radio astronomy, they had this massive, big horn thing set up to hear the sounds that stars make."

"How would we make a horn like that?" EDDIE asked, "Would that take a long time?"

"Nah, you're right, it'd take forever, and I don't have enough pocket money to buy batteries to keep you going that long!"

When he heard that news, EDDIE did his best to look glum, which wasn't easy for a little robot.

"Besides, Mum would shoot me if I started building something that big in the back yard," Crafty said. "I'd have to get rid of the clothesline for starters. I don't think she'd be very happy about that ..."

Suddenly Crafty slipped off the stool he was sitting on. "I have an absolutely brilliant idea," he said.

Chapter 3

C rafty crossed the shed where he started rummaging through his dad's odds and ends cupboard. It was where everything, absolutely everything no one knew what to do with eventually found a home. That included those things that still worked and might be useful again, no one knew when, but sometime in the future, that was for sure. Until that day arrived, they had all settled on a shelf for a comfortable holiday in their dusty jackets.

"I knew Dad hadn't thrown you out!" Crafty exclaimed. After lots of clattering, and muttering and impromptu rearranging, and even more muttering and lots of "I'll sort you out later," from Crafty, one of the shelves, seemingly limitless in depth and capacity, gave up an almost forgotten treasure, reluctantly, sadly, but with a sense of inevitability.   Crafty pulled his head from the cupboard, swiped a clump of dust from the end of his nose, and brandished a battered up old radio set.

"Grandpa's old shortwave!" He declared. "We'll get this rigged up quick time, easy as eating breakfast."

EDDIE thought that must be very wise, but he was puzzled. "Crafty, what is breakfast?"

"Breakfast? Oh, EDDIE," Crafty said kindly, "Robots don't eat breakfast."

"They don't?" EDDIE asked, sounding disappointed. When you are young, and when you are a special kind of robot who needs to know all sorts of things to solve puzzles and infer lots of stuff from the data you digest, not knowing what breakfast was, and worse, not being able to experience breakfast for yourself seemed a bit of an oversight.

"No. They don't need to. Robots don't have stomachs."

"Oh." EDDIE tried to look down to where he thought his stomach should be. "But you said eating breakfast was easy?"

"It is if you have a stomach. And besides," Crafty went on, "If you had a stomach and you could eat breakfast, or lunch or anything else for that matter, we wouldn't need to work out how to boost your power, we'd just feed you! Which I guess, in a way, is what we are trying to do."

"Oh," EDDIE said again. He knew it should make sense, but it didn't. If he had a stomach he'd know about breakfast. It wouldn't be something he'd worry about. It would be something he did.

"Crafty?"

"Yes EDDIE?" Crafty was not paying EDDIE much attention. He had removed the radio's back panel and was peering intently at the circuitry.

"What's the radio for again?"

"You really shouldn't skip breakfast," Crafty said. "It's the most important meal of the day, and if you skip it, you struggle to think straight. It's clear to me, EDDIE, because you aren't thinking straight, you're obviously not getting enough of the right nutrition." Crafty was instantly sorry for teasing EDDIE, and he was sorry he brought up the subject of food. His stomach growled, reminding him he was hungry, and it was creeping up on dinner time.

He looked over to where the little robot sat almost forlornly, and he smiled kindly at him.

"I'm sorry, EDDIE, I'm teasing you. Perhaps I should explain," Crafty began, "My plan is to make this radio into a sort of listening horn."

"That's good, I think."

"If we can set this up to receive that carrier signal I mentioned," Crafty explained, prodding at something in the back of the radio with his favourite screwdriver. "It's all about energy received and energy converted. If we tap into the right frequency, we might be able to amplify the current enough and use it to boost your power. Or even better, power you wirelessly. No batteries needed!"

"Will that work?" EDDIE sounded doubtful.

"I have no idea. But around here we never say never!"

Crafty went back to the odds and ends cupboard. He hefted out an old cardboard box full of bits and pieces and spare parts and unidentifiable things he was hoping to find a use for some day; when he worked out what they were, that is. This was his secret stash, set apart from the other bric-a-brac, bibs, bobs and all that forgotten stuff in the cupboard. After a few minutes of rummaging, Crafty looked up, disappointed.

"Nuh. Not what we need. Not even close." He started chewing on a fingernail, thinking hard. "What can I use? There must be something? Maybe ... I wonder if that would work? I mean, we could give it a go and see. Even if it was just proof of concept. Yes, yes, it might just work."

EDDIE was learning that sometimes it was better to let Crafty run with his thoughts. If Crafty needed his input, EDDIE was sure he'd ask for it, and that in time EDDIE would be able to interpret the hints Crafty gave as to when that might be. EDDIE didn't know any other inventors, of course, but it seemed interrupting them when they are thinking through a problem wasn't such a great idea, even if he was an *inference* engine and might find some bit or morsel of information to complete the puzzle at hand.

"Kitchen," Crafty declared suddenly, then chuckled. "Oh, that's sweet! This is going to require stealth, and I mean real *deep* stealth."

EDDIE sat quietly on the workbench, looking more bemused than before.

"Wait here," Crafty whispered.

"I wasn't planning on going anywhere," EDDIE said softly.

But in his mind's eye Crafty was firing up his cloaking device. He had a plan. All he had to do was execute it.

Quietly, without another word to EDDIE, he slipped out of the shed.

Chapter 4

T he stretch of yard between the shed door and the back of the house had telescoped out to several grassy kilometres. Crafty couldn't remember it being that far.

Ever.

If his mother happened to look out of the upstairs window at the wrong time, he was a goner. He had to risk it. He couldn't see another way of solving the power problem.

He could feel the tension in his shoulders and in his legs. He knew he had to move fast, stay low, and find cover. But there wasn't an opportunity to conceal himself between here and the back of the house. He could use the washing on the clothesline to hide his approach, but that was about it. Crafty had to work on the idea that if someone was focused on something else, if they weren't looking for you, then they wouldn't notice you were there; technically, you'd be invisible.

"On the count of three ..." Crafty breathed.

"One ... two ... three ..."

As fast as he could, which wasn't very fast, thanks to too many custard tarts, he sprinted for the clothesline. And stopped, still as a stone. He scrunched down under the sheets as they slowly billowed in the lazy afternoon breeze. His short burst of intense energy had left him breathless. Or was it his asthma? He pushed his glasses back up his sweaty nose and peeked out under the sheets. It wouldn't be too long before his mother gave him a yell and asked him to bring these in, and don't forget to fold them, neatly, and put the pegs back into the basket! Neatly!

Just one more short burst of speed, and I am there, Crafty thought. *I can do this.* He closed his eyes and bunched up his meagre supply of courage.

A clumsy forward roll brought him clear of the sheets, then, with a steel-spring leap he was off.

In a sweaty panting instant he was at the back door.

Made it, he thought. "Crafty to base," he whispered to no one in particular. "I have completed the first part of the mission. There is no sign of hostiles."

As quietly as he could, he eased open the screen door and slipped into the kitchen. He blinked rapidly, waiting those long agonising seconds for his eyes to adjust from the bright afternoon light to the relative gloom inside the house. He had to be careful to maintain full stealth mode. The slightest sound could reveal his position. The last thing he wanted was to bump into something, or worse, someone.

If he was caught now that would be it before dinner, it would all be over, he would be given some chore to do, then it would be homework, music practice, and into the bath. There was no way he'd be able to sneak back out to the shed before EDDIE's power failed completely.

But the kitchen was empty.

He could hear his mother moving around upstairs. In the front room the television had been left on, and some game show audience was shouting encouragement to the contestant. That was good, it would muffle any tiny noise he might make.

He crouched low and with protesting thighs, duck-walked to the pot cupboard. Slowly he opened it and peered in.

Saucepans, frying pans and Dad's favourite cheese grater, cylindrical and rusty. There were lids that didn't belong to anything, and pots and containers that should have had lids but didn't. Somewhere along the line it had all forgotten what it was supposed to be and where it lived.

"I know it's in here somewhere," Crafty whispered to himself. Carefully he reached into the back of the cupboard and began to feel around. *"It's gotta be here,"* he thought.

"Where ... are ... you?"

He froze as his searching hand pushed the non-stick fry pan up against the soup pot.

There was sudden silence upstairs.

"Don't come down... don't come down," Crafty pleaded under his breath.

Moment's dragged by. Finally, his mother moved, the floor creaking beneath her ... still in the bedroom.

He let out the breath he hadn't realised he was holding.

"It *has* to be here somewhere."

Then, as he was about to give up, and fall back on Plan B, whatever Plan B was, his fingertips brushed against the polished steel petals of his prize.

"Gotcha!"

But this mission wasn't over yet.

First, he had to ease his prize past the cheese grater and the flour sifter, through the obstacle course of pots and lids and out into the afternoon light. Finally, his heart hammering in his chest loud enough to be heard next door, he had what he came for. With a glance down the hall he padded softly to the pantry, and deftly hooked the roll of aluminium foil from the middle shelf.

"Done," Crafty declared in a whisper, "Mission complete, returning to base."

Still in full stealth mode, he slipped out of the house, and back to the shed.

*****

"You were gone an awfully long time," EDDIE said when Crafty finally made an appearance through the shed door.

"Do you think?" Crafty said trying to sound nonchalant, which was difficult as his heart was still pounding from the adrenaline. "It can't have been more than a few minutes. I think it always feels longer when you are waiting for something."

EDDIE took a moment to check his system clock. His batteries were starting to fade again. Slowing everything was running down. He was losing time. Or was it a system fault. His internal clock kept resetting to 00:00:00. He didn't want to alarm Crafty as he worked on a solution to the problem, but it wouldn't be long before he wound down completely, the gentle green glow of his micro-dot-camera eyes fading to black.

"What's that for?" EDDIE asked, trying to keep his neural processors from thinking about the inevitable. He could see what Crafty was holding, but EDDIE had no idea what it was. After several moments of searching his still limited databases, and finding nothing to reference it against, EDDIE decided he'd wait and see exactly what it was Crafty had in mind.

"Give me a minute or maybe two, and all will be revealed," Crafty said, as if to validate EDDIE's strategy of patience. "It's just what we need to go with Grandpa's old short-wave radio."

"Crafty, what's short-wave?" EDDIE was not trying to be unhelpful by deliberately interrupting Crafty as he did his work, but EDDIE's brimming curiosity prompted him to ask.

"I remember sitting and listening to ham radio broadcasts on this when Grandpa was still alive," Crafty said wistfully, not really answering EDDIE's question. He missed his grandpa. Grandpa always had time to spend with Crafty. Crafty's dad was always at work, either up at the hospital or out on call looking after someone who was sick. Crafty thought it was neat that his dad cared for sick people, he didn't begrudge him that, he just wished that they could spend more time together.

Mindful of EDDIE's fading power, Crafty arranged the tools he needed on the bench: screwdrivers, wire strippers, flux, his soldering iron, and some spare parts; transistors, capacitors, a diode or two just in case.

EDDIE emitted a short, distressed bleep. "Time is getting to be very much of the essence, Crafty."

"Then let's not waste any!" Crafty said and set to work.

He deftly wrapped the old-style vegetable steamer with foil and soldered wires to each of its four metal legs. He paused for a moment, staring intently into the guts of the radio, ignoring his glasses as they slid down his nose for the hundredth time that afternoon. "Got it!" he declared and with a confident hand wielded the soldering iron.

"That should do it," Crafty said. He plugged the radio into one of the power sockets on the wall at the back of the work bench. He let out a long slow breath and reached across to flip the switch.

Suddenly he stopped.

"What is it?" asked EDDIE. "What's wrong?" His power was fading fast, and he was feeling ever more desperate. He knew that his time was running out.

"What if this doesn't work?" Crafty asked, echoing EDDIE's exact thoughts, and EDDIE could hear the nervousness in his voice.

"Then I remain on battery, and we find another way!"

Chapter 5

This must work! If it doesn't..." Crafty's voice caught in his throat. "The batteries will eventually fail, and your capacitors will discharge and when they do, we'll lose all your programming."

EDDIE let out a little squeak. "But you can reprogram me ... can't you?"

"I could, but you might not be the *you* you are now," Crafty said, solemnly. "You see, the longer you are powered on, and processing data, receiving input, the more you are making neural connections. Your mind is growing EDDIE. Growing all the time. With every thought you have. I don't want to lose that! I don't want to lose *you*."

"Best you turn it on and see what happens then..." EDDIE said as brightly as he could manage.

Crafty drew in a long slow deep breath. The world seemed to stop turning as his fingers brushed against the power switch. Decisively he pressed it down. Its click was unexpectedly extra loud and filled the empty, suddenly cavernous space of the shed.

And nothing happened ...

And then, slowly, as if waking up from a long sleep, the dial on the old radio began to glow and the sound of static came from its dusty speakers.

"I am sorry Crafty," EDDIE said slowly, "I don't feel anything."

"Not yet!" Crafty cried. "We have to tune it in. We have to find the right frequency. We have to secure just the right signal."

Little by little Crafty began to turn the big black knob on the front of the radio. The sound of static changed, rising and falling as the indicator moved in slow, precise increments, and then, when the pointer was passed halfway along the gauge, something happened.

Or, more precisely three things happened. The static from the radio turned into a low hum, the petals of the veggie steamer began to glow a deep emerald green, and EDDIE let out an alarmed squawk.

"Crafty..." EDDIE said, his tiny electronic voice trembling.

More carefully now, Crafty turned the dial. The hum grew louder, and the veggie steamer glowed brighter.

"Crafty ..." EDDIE began again. "I don't feel well."

Something crackled, filling the air with the sound of rice puffs. There was a loud BOOM. The foundations of the shed and every other part of it shook and rattled and it was all lit up with flashes of blinding green light.

And EDDIE toppled sideways onto the work bench, with a thump, and his little sound bar began emitting tiny peeps of stereophonic distress. There was a long, loud, graunching whir. The radio fell silent. The veggie steamer settled to a soft phosphorescent glow.

EDDIE lay perfectly still. Smoke puffed in thin tendrils from his joints and from his micro-dot-camera eyes and from underneath his battery compartment cover.

"EDDIE?" said Crafty, leaning over him. "*EDDIE!?*"

Crafty hardly dared to touch him. There seemed to be a layer of green light shimmering across his silver skin.

"EDDIE?"

"Functioning." EDDIE said. His voice sounded ... different. Not as small, and not as electronic. "What is an hypotenuse?"

"EDDIE?"

"I thought I knew. Perhaps I did once. Is it some sort of pottery? No? Can you cook with it?"

"EDDIE?"

"I think it might be connected somehow to the square root of possum snot."

"EDDIE?"

"Ooooh. I feel yucky."

"I'm not surprised," Crafty agreed. "But you do seem to be functioning."

"I really have no idea."

"Seriously?"

"Crafty?" EDDIE said, shaking himself with a rattle like screws in a jar.

"Yes?"

"I might have something loose; my calibration feels like it's way off..."

"Yes?"

"Oh, and I don't know whether you have noticed..."

"No, I probably haven't. Noticed what?"

"We are not alone..."

"Huh?" Crafty looked around sharply. "What do you mean ... we're not alone?"

EDDIE managed to raise a slightly singed arm, which he hadn't been able to do before. He flexed a silicone tipped metal forefinger toward the shed door.

Hardly daring to breathe, Crafty turned to see what EDDIE was pointing at.

Sitting on the floor, thumping the side of its head with a webbed hand was ...

"What on earth is *THAT*!?"

At the sound of Crafty's voice the creature seemed to gather its wits. It turned its seaweed-coloured glance toward them. "Muk'Vuh!!" It exclaimed emphatically and promptly hopped through the cat flap at the bottom of the door.

*****

In the lingering silence that followed, Crafty could hear the gentle clacking chatter of EDDIE's relays. "After it!" Crafty cried. He was at the shed door in a blur of movement. He threw it open to the now thinning afternoon light. In an instant he was out in the vast, silent, empty backyard. Frantically, he looked around. "Where'd it go?"

Beside him, Crafty heard a soft clank. He glanced down to where EDDIE was standing, uncertain of legs that were still new and a bit unsteady. For a moment Crafty thought of a baby giraffe wobbling all over the place before it got its balance.

"Which way?" Crafty asked. "Which way?" His desperation was rising. Somewhere in the backyard was … goodness only knew. He'd never seen a creature like it.

And it was almost dinner time! Any second his mother would call him, and he'd have to respond pronto.

No sooner had Crafty thought this than there was a long, loud, echoing YOWL.

"Was that the *cat*?"

"Thruk'Vik! Yek vah." A green, gurgly voice matched the volume of the hissing cat. "Nak'chuk! Shal'gak! Ich mak yuk!!"

The cat howled. There was another throaty green gurgle. The scramble of claws filled the air, and the cat slid into view around the corner of the shed and came to a shuddering, undignified stop.

"Oh, for goodness sake, stop gaping and catch it!" the cat said.

Crafty's mouth, which had been hanging open wider than a farm gate, clapped shut with an audible thunk.

"Oh, would you cut it out!" the cat said. "For someone as smart as you are, William Ambrose Craft, sometimes you can be incredibly THICK!"

Crafty was shaking his head as if something had come loose, and he was expecting it to rattle.

"It tried to eat me!" the cat growled. "What was I supposed to do? I smacked its nose. If it wasn't happy before, it certainly isn't happy now!"

Crafty's mouth fell open again.

"Stop gaping!" said the cat. "I told you, it tried to eat me."

Crafty continued to gape.

"Crafty," EDDIE said hopefully. "Do cat's talk?" He wasn't sure his question was going to break through Crafty's astonishment.

Crafty's mouth opened and closed like a guppies.

"*Do* cats talk?" EDDIE asked again.

"Ahhhh...."

"I don't think cats talk," EDDIE concluded, too brightly for Crafty's liking.

"Right when we need him most, he has lost it," said the cat, eyes boring into Crafty as if somehow that might bring him to his senses.

"I'm sure of it. Cat's ... do ... not ... talk ..." EDDIE said, his relays clacking emphatically.

"Well, *this* cat certainly DOES!" the cat harrumphed.

EDDIE almost seemed to shake his head.

"Oh, don't you start!" the cat snapped at EDDIE. "You are quite right. Cats can't talk, but *I* can."

"Who are you?" asked Crafty, finally finding his voice.

"If you aren't the cat?" EDDIE added after a pause.

"*I* am Mrs McKenzie," said the cat, as if that answered everything.

This statement was followed by a very, very long silence.

"I might need to reprogram," EDDIE muttered.

"We have a flippy-floppy green mutant froggy-lizard thing on the loose and you are worried about your *programming*?" Mrs McKenzie said.

"I'm confused," said Crafty.

"*You're* confused?" said EDDIE.

"And I am Mrs McKenzie," said the cat. "And for the moment that's all you need to know."

EDDIE emitted a low distressed squeak. "Someone has scrambled my processors."

"Scrambled with bacon?" asked Mrs McKenzie mischievously. "Oh, I love bacon."

"EDDIE, get a grip," Crafty said. "We can't afford you blowing a valve."

"We are wasting time!" Mrs McKenzie pointed out.

"I'm not moving until I know what's going on," Crafty said.

"Me either," said EDDIE, and tried to cross his arms.

The cat, or Mrs McKenzie, or whoever it was, huffed loudly. "Oh, have it your way. But we need to be quick. The cat gets me to where I need to be. Now, let me tell you, I *do not* like cats, not at all, they are snooty, and their breath smells like fish. And I can't even begin to describe how bad kibble tastes! When they said to me, I would have to be a cat, well, what I said to them was not at all polite, so I won't repeat it. But, you see, we couldn't use the dog. He is just not smart enough. He's a boof head." The cat made a wheezing, laughing sound. "Or is that woof head?!"

"Ah, I crack myself up sometimes! Look, if you feel just under my neck, you will find a small lump. That's the neural transmitter. An implant. It is wired into the cat's brain so I can control what it does and where it goes, and it lets me communicate with you."

"How do you see?" asked EDDIE.

"Nano-cameras," Mrs McKenzie said. "I just hope she never has to sneeze."

"You put cameras up her *nose?*" Crafty said.

"Of course. Where else would you put them?"

"What happens if you want to look behind you?" EDDIE's curiosity seemed genuine.

"I turn around!" The cat's calico tail gave an annoyed flick.

"Why not link into her optic nerves?" Crafty asked enthusiastically, his mind turning over the possibilities.

"We haven't quite perfected that technology yet. We will. It's just a matter of time."

EDDIE made a graunching noise.

"Yes?" Mrs McKenzie asked, turning her gaze upon EDDIE. "You have something to add?"

"Our escapee," observed EDDIE, "Is escaping..."

Chapter 6

Mrs McKenzie padded gingerly to the corner of the shed and peered around.

"Do you see anything?" Crafty asked in a whisper.

Mrs McKenzie harrumphed a second time and flicked the cat's tail. "No."

"If you suddenly found yourself on a strange planet," asked EDDIE "What would *you* do?"

Crafty had been tapping his front teeth with a fingernail, deep in thought. Suddenly he stopped and looked down at EDDIE. "Wait. What? What did you say? You think this this is an *alien*? As in extra-terrestrial not of this world but from another planet in another galaxy type alien *alien*?"

"It's ugly enough," observed Mrs McKenzie, tartly.

"Well ..." EDDIE said slowly. "Given the evidence we have, taking time to make an analysis of its behaviour patterns, the patterns we have observed so far at least ... what else could it be?"

"This isn't *Independence Day*!" Crafty said, sounding agitated.

"Crafty," EDDIE said evenly, "What conclusion would you have me make? I am an *inference* engine after all. That's what you made to do. Right?"

"Meantime," interrupted Mrs McKenzie tersely, "As EDDIE has rightly pointed out. Our one and only once in a lifetime, totally unique, never before and hitherto unknown alien creature is making good its gooey, green flippy-floppy and very unpleasant escape!!!"

EDDIE sighed. "First Contact," he said, "And it's getting away."

"I'll give *it* first contact," muttered Mrs McKenzie, not very kindly.

"I think you already did," EDDIE said.

Mrs McKenzie gave EDDIE a look that would have melted a lesser alloy. "Meantime..." She said, sounding annoyed at the prospect of having to repeat herself. "It is getting away..."

"Oh! Yes, after it!" Crafty shouted.

EDDIE gave a little chirrup and stepped out into the open expanse of the backyard. He wondered for a moment if this is what they meant by finding your sea legs? At least he wasn't wobbling all over the place anymore.

"Which way did it go? Maybe it's like a chameleon and can camouflage itself," Crafty said. "Mrs McKenzie, can you smell it? I mean can you sniff it out for us?"

Mrs McKenzie swished her tail. "I, young William Craft, am *not* a dog."

Her tone stopped Crafty in his tracks.

"With nano-cameras implanted in the olfactory system I dare say the cat's sense of smell would be reduced..." EDDIE clanked to silence as Mrs McKenzie's withering gaze once again turned his way.

"EDDIE," managed Crafty. "Can you please go infra-red?"

"Yes! Of course," crowed Mrs McKenzie, "Heat signatures."

"I have infra-red?" EDDIE sounded nonplussed.

"Yes," said Crafty, "And night vision."

"Infra-red, hmm, nice," Mrs McKenzie commented. "Unless of course it's cold blooded."

"That's not very helpful." The desperation was starting to show in Crafty's voice. He wasn't as worried about the alien creature loose in the backyard as he was about his mother choosing that moment to come out of the house, catching them mid-adventure. She wouldn't be impressed at all if their visitor flippy-flopped up to her and gave her a big, sloppy, wet hello. Crafty shook his head, trying to unsee that picture.

"I see it!" EDDIE broke the silence.

Crafty pushed his glasses back up his nose and squinted as if that would help his focus. "Where?"

"It is standing at the far corner of the yard. It is over near the compost heap. Currently it is sniffing last night's salad."

"Oh great, it's vegetarian," Mrs McKenzie sniffed.

"It can't be vegetarian; we know it likes cat." Crafty rubbed his chin in thought. "That's it!" He exclaimed.

"What is?" Mrs McKenzie asked, sounding uncertain.

"It likes cats."

"Oh no. No. No no no. Get that thought right out of your head, young man... I will not have it!"

Crafty hadn't known it was possible for a cat to stomp its foot, until that moment.

"I ... will ... not ... have ... it!"

EDDIE looked quizzically up at Crafty. He wasn't sure what Crafty had in mind.

"I was going to suggest we use Mrs McKenzie to lure our friend, this Muk'Vuh into a trap," Crafty explained. "And once we do ..." Crafty was jiggling with excitement, having followed his thought through to its logical conclusion.

"I simply *won't* be used as bait, young man!" Mrs McKenzie's tone was razor sharp.

Crafty was thinking fast. He realised he was grabbing at the most obvious solution. It wasn't going to happen if Mrs McKenzie didn't cooperate. A cranky cat is not something to be trifled with.

"Then ...we ... um ... we ..."

"We find another way to send it back to where it came from," EDDIE said, finishing the thought for him.

"Mean time, our new friend seems to have ideas of his own," Mrs McKenzie observed.

The creature had flippy-flopped its happy-hoppy way across the backyard and was investigating the dog's bowl. It sniffed all around the dog food that was resting like day old casserole in the bottom of the dish. It gave the brown mush a huge appreciative whiff. Tilting its head sideways, it gave an experimental flick with its turquoise tongue.

"You know," said EDDIE as he observed the creature, "I think it's kind of cute in a froggy-mutant-lizard kind of way."

Mrs McKenzie harrumphed and shook her calico head in disagreement.

There was a shake of the creature's spiky crested head, a wrinkle of the nose, and its thin caterpillar lips curled back from teeth that looked way too sharp, even from this distance.

"Yeeeeech," the creature said. It seemed to weave where it stood, eyes closed, lost in rapture at the taste and smell of the dog food.

In that moment, Kepler, who had been asleep in his kennel flicked open his left eye and still a bit groggy, took several long moments to process that there was a strange critter standing near his dinner bowl.

"Grrr?"

"Grargl." The intruder flicked out its tongue, once again testing the dog food. With one slippery gulp it sucked the entire messy brown lump into its mouth.

"Ech'nek yu'yak bla'ach," it said as if in the deepest approval. And it looked around for more.

Kepler, not liking this turn of events at all, crept forward, commando style, head low, left lip half curled to show a lazy fang; if he had been a braver dog he might have growled. But deep down he was used to naps and tummy rubs and chewing old slippers and stray underwear rather than dealing with strange otherworldly flippy-floppy froggy-mutant-lizard creatures that somehow didn't seem to fit his perfect knowledge of the backyard.

The flippy-floppy green visitor sensed Kepler's approach and turned. It tilted its head to one side, then the other. "Ke'ch gruk?" It sounded puzzled. "Yeee juk!"

Kepler barked twice, and then launched himself forward, his teeth bared. In the same instant the unfamiliar green intruder shot upward, avoiding Kepler's bite by the barest of margins. Kepler's jaws clapped shut on empty air.

There was a yowl, Crafty wasn't sure from whom, and somehow their not so little green guest was on Kepler's back. It had grabbed a thick chunk of Kepler's fur in its froggy hand and was trying to hang on for its flippy-floppy life with everything it had. Kepler became a wild bucking bronco of a dog. He leaped and spun and turned and jumped, trying to dislodge this unwanted passenger, all the while howling and snarling and snapping.

"Shd'ekk yee gaa'kak," the Muk'Vuh hollered, almost as if it were enjoying itself. "Yach'oooo!"

Kepler howled, and bolted blindly, desperately forward gathering supreme speed.

"Oh noooo," Crafty cried.

But it was way too late.

The dog slid to an almost catastrophic halt millimetres from the back fence. The now terrified Muk'Vuh did the only thing it could.

It let go.

At the same time the dog gave one last Herculean lift of his haunches, and a whip flick of his tail, as if to say good riddance.

And launched the unwanted jockey in an almost perfect arc...

Up...

Up...

Up...

... and over the back fence, a gooey-green silhouette against the deep blue of the afternoon sky.

The creature turned a less than delicate tumbling somersault with pike straight into Mr Robinson's swimming pool, as Mr Robinson happily sidestroked his way back to the shallow end for his glasses and towel.

"Oh crikey..." Crafty groaned.

"For goodness sake, do something," Mrs McKenzie urged. "Do *anything*."

"What ....?"

"Don't look at me," Mrs McKenzie said. "I don't swim!"

Crafty eyes scanned Mr Robinson's backyard. What could he do, what could he use to get the Muk'Vuh out of the pool and into custody. Left to right to left his gaze went.

Ah!

The leaf net.

Not normally athletic, but high on a body hit of pure adrenaline, Crafty vaulted the fence, landing in almost perfect superhero pose, losing his glasses as he did. He scrabbled in the grass for his glasses and lit quickly for the saggy old leaf net that had been thrown across the sun lounge, half in the shade of Mr Robinson's Balinese gazebo.

The Muk'Vuh was happily flapping and splashing. It hadn't yet spotted Mr Robinson. Nor had Mr Robinson, blind as a bat without his glasses, spotted the Muk'Vuh.

Feeling the need for stealth, Crafty took hold of the leaf net in a white knuckled grip and edged as slowly and carefully as he could towards the pool's edge. The last thing he wanted was to add to the problem by falling in.

The Muk'Vuh was the image of perfect bliss, lost in the joy of the water. Crafty lowered the net into the pool, sidling forward and then sideways, trying to find the right moment to place the net under the Muk'Vuh for a quick scoop and getaway.

Then everything went pear-shaped.

Turning to float on his back, Mr Robinson peered uncertainly towards the deep end of the pool where he could just make out the shape of someone, standing with the leaf net, brandished....

"Young William? Is that you? What are you up to over there?"

"Oh … um … I wanted to help clean your pool … leaves and stuff … you know?"

The Muk'Vuh wasn't slow. It had spotted Crafty out of the corner of its eye. Perhaps it felt the presence of the net. Crafty didn't know. But it barrel-rolled in the water and with one powerful push of its hind flippers it propelled itself at considerable speed straight towards Mr Robinson.

"Oh no…" Crafty groaned again. "That's *not* good."

Mr Robinson spotted the Muk'Vuh at the same time the Muk'Vuh spotted him.

"William! Quick. The net." Mr Robinson tried his best to swim away from the Muk'Vuh, but the inevitable happened.

The Muk'Vuh let out a thick throaty gurgle and buried its flippy-froggy fingers deep into the thick curly black hair that grew all over Mr Robinson's back and shoulders. Mr Robinson wanted none of that, he tried to reach back far enough to disentangle the creature.   But the Muk'Vuh clung on, limpet-tight, at least for a few moments.

Until a great matted tuft of Mr Robinson gave way.

The Muk'Vuh squeaked its surprise, flew backwards in an almost perfect arc, straight into the net Crafty had at the ready.

"Got you!" He cried, chest filling with triumph. "I got you."

He gave the net a deft twist, just as his grandpa had shown him after landing a fish, and with a wave to Mr Robinson, he hurdled back over the fence into the safety of his own backyard.

Chapter 7

W ow, that was way too close," Crafty said. He was bent forward, hands on his knees, trying to catch the breath he had lost from the effort of finding the superpowers needed to vault the fence and from the sheer, gut-wrenching tension of the last few minutes.

The gooey-green visitor, wrapped firmly in the saggy leaf net, had decided escape was no longer an option and had stopped wriggling.

"Yeg mech, oog ak chk!" it said, glaring up at Crafty. He had to admit, he didn't like the tone of its gaze.

"You weigh a tonne," Crafty told it and half carried, half dragged it to the front of the shed. "And what's more, you smell disgusting."

"William?"

"Oh great!" Crafty groaned. "Not now, please not now."

"William?!" He could see his mother's shadow at the back door.

"Yes Mum?"

"Is everything all right?"

"Yes Mum. Why wouldn't it be?"

"I thought I heard a loud noise."

"It's all good Mum."

"So long as you are all right. I have to go out, for a while, I'm sorry. Mrs Bird's had a fall."

"Oh. That's terrible!" Crafty's heart gave a leap. Mrs Bird was elderly and lived on her own. His Mum did her best to look out for her, but Mrs Bird was frail, and none too steady on her feet. As often as he could, Crafty would help by mowing Mrs Birds' grass, and doing whatever other odd jobs he was asked to do. No questions. No grumbling. He liked Mrs Bird a lot. She gave him pieces of home made slice and cookies and glasses of ice-cold milk. And besides, there would be nothing worse than being old and alone with no family living close by when you needed help. It really was the least he could do.

"OK," Crafty called back. "Oh, and Mum, can you please tell Mrs Bird I'm thinking of her?"

"Shall do. And if I'm not back, there are leftovers you can heat for dinner."

"You bet. Thanks Mum."

"And William?"

"Yes Mum?"

"Do your homework!"

"Yes Mum."

Crafty felt as if he'd dodged an artillery salvo, but he was still concerned for Mrs Bird.

"Shug nech." The Muk'Vuh's weird, croaky voice brought him sharply back to the current dilemma.

Crafty slowly let out a long breath. "What are we going to do with you?" he said. "Whatever *you* are."

The shed door had been left open, and as best he could, wrestling with the weight of the Muk'Vuh, Crafty pushed it wider with his foot and stepped inside. EDDIE and Mrs McKenzie slipped into the gloomy interior of the shed behind him.

With a mighty heave Crafty lifted the leaf net and its captive onto the work bench.

"Yug nuch, ach nech."

"My thoughts exactly."

*****

Leaning on the workbench, Crafty was tapping its surface with a fingertip. His eyes were firmly fixed on the creature wrapped in the leaf net, and its gooey seaweed eyes were firmly fixed on him.

It did not seem impressed.

EDDIE was looking from boy to critter and back, whilst Mrs McKenzie was content for the moment, to sit and allow the cat to clean a paw with her raspy tongue.

"If it came in on the carrier wave," Crafty said to no one in particular. "It can go back out the same way."

If EDDIE had eyebrows, he would certainly have raised one.

"You see," Crafty continued to explain, "This old radio set isn't just a receiver, it's also a transmitter. It was pretty advanced for its time. Although, Grandpa was always tinkering with things like this."

EDDIE blipped; it was his electronic version of a nod.

"The frequencies will be identical. We just have to work out a way to ramp up the signal strength to send our friend here back to where he came from."

"Shuk juk, nek yech," said the Muk'Vuh sounding despondent. Perhaps it was thinking about the joyous taste of dog food and wasn't impressed with the idea of being sent home.

"We don't have a power source anything like that, Crafty," EDDIE said.

"Or do we?" Crafty looking at EDDIE intently.

"Hmmm...." EDDIE's cooling fan whirred hard as if in nervous response.

"It hadn't occured to me until now," Crafty said. "But you were running on batteries until ..."

"What's your point?" Mrs McKenzie asked, looking up from the cat's paw cleaning.

"The green flash."

"The green flash?"

"Yes."

"EDDIE, come here a sec," Crafty said.

EDDIE reluctantly complied, and Crafty took hold of him, gently, and laid him on his side.

EDDIE yipped.

"What's wrong?" Crafty asked with genuine concern.

"Your hands are *cold!*"

Crafty selected a screwdriver and popped open EDDIE's access cover. Almost instantly the relative gloom of the shed was filled with a steady, neon-green light.

Grabbing Grandpa's magnifying glass, Crafty peered into EDDIE's internal cavity, which was crammed full of circuitry and the valves that glowed ...

"Green..."

Mrs McKenzie, back in control of Helix, padded along the bench, avoiding the Muk'Vuh as widely as she could, and with a wrinkled nose tried her best to peer inside EDDIE.

"Move you hand," she said to Crafty, "I can't see."

For a long time, Mrs McKenzie gazed into EDDIE's innards, as if mesmerised by the soft pulsating green. "Amazing work, William Craft, truly amazing.

"It is possible EDDIE's core frequency is the same as the receiver," Mrs McKenzie stated. "Or whatever it is that is driving the signal from the other end. If we reversed the polarity, we could boost the signal enough ... Or you could set up a line array."

"And with the signal boost that might just be enough. Brilliant! EDDIE, you are about to be our power source."

EDDIE did not like the sound of that at all.

With Mum away, the coast was clear and stealth mode was unnecessary. Crafty bolted for the kitchen. He came back with several different sized pot lids and an industrial-sized roll of aluminium foil he had gratefully discovered at the back of the pantry. He had used up the other roll wrapping the veggie steamer.

Quickly, with his brow crinkled in deep concentration, he set about lining the pot lids with foil, and linking them with wire. He set them in a semi-circle, careful to align them with the original antenna.

The Muk'Vuh watched him with intent, gooey green eyes.

In a moment Crafty grunted his satisfaction and stepped back.

"That's as good as I can make it."

Without any ceremony at all Crafty took hold of EDDIE and with deft strokes of the soldering iron ran wires from the array to EDDIE and then to the back of the receiver. EDDIE suppressing a chirrup of alarm, lay quietly on his back, his arms and legs hanging limp. If he had learned anything during his short operational life it was to trust Crafty.

"OK, that should do it."

Crafty grabbed the Muk'Vuh, and, still wrapped in the leaf net, plonked it in the middle of the antenna array. It made a soft, squishy noise of discontent.

"Are we ready?"

Checking the dial on the receiver, Crafty flipped the switch to "Send" and waited.

Out of EDDIE's internal cavity came a soft whirring sound, and an even stronger green glow filled the shed. They hardly noticed it at first, but there was a new sound, a low frequency hum, which provided an accompaniment to EDDIE's whir. It was a hum that grew louder and higher in tone until with an ear-splitting ZIP the air crackled and sparked, green and blue and yellow, like an aurora.

Then, there was a huge flash, followed by a deep, resonating silence.

Crafty and Mrs McKenzie blinked furiously to clear their offended vision.

When they were able to focus enough to look around, they saw that the Muk'Vuh had gone.

The leaf net, although slightly singed, was otherwise undamaged and completely empty.

And where EDDIE had been lying bare moments ago, was nothing but a large black scorch mark.

Chapter 8

E DDIE lay on something that felt both soft and coarse at the same time. It surprised him he could feel it at all, as he wasn't programmed for physical sensation.

Everything around him was dark. He was trying hard to reset his vision sensors. He was having trouble moving. Something prevented him from sitting up.

"Gech..."

It was an unpleasant, yet familiar sound.

"Gha'ach ..."

He felt the sudden heat of breath. With it came a smell, all wet, and rancid, like old dog food mixed with decomposing seaweed.

"Shuch, da'gech nah!"

EDDIE trembled at the threat in those words. He couldn't suppress the tweep of distress that leaked from his speakers.

"Fth'ach," The Muk'Vuh said, its drool splashing caustically on EDDIE's casing. After the longest time lying very, very still, with his vision sensors clamped tight shut against what he didn't want to see, EDDIE realised the creature was gone.

He let out a long hssss that he hoped sounded like a sigh and released those parts of him he had clenched. He was lying on his back, staring up at a sky that was the wrong colour: it was orange and brown rather than the endless blue sky of home.

He took a moment to wipe the goop off as best he could, rubbing his face in the grass. It felt weird but it did the job. Everything was blurred and wispy at first, doubled up and out of focus, but slowly things became clear.

Subconsciously his sensors ran through their usual checks: atmosphere, humidity, barometric pressure, a dozen other tests that gave him a sense of where he was.

And where he wasn't.

There was nothing but silence, and the sense that he was a long way from home. And he was alone.

After a time, he managed to sit up. He felt his power drain, and it was slow to recover. He was on a grassy hillside that gently lowered itself down into a valley through which a narrow stream trickled. The stream glinted, doing its best to reflect the orange sky.

All around him, scattered on the yellowish grass were green flecks, like seed pods, or gemstones. He ran another quick power check. The residual weakness he felt did not surprise him; chasing a Muk'Vuh was hard work. Yet everything seemed to be holding, at least for the moment. "*That's reassuring,*" he said to himself. He had enough power to walk. But which way should he go? And what would he do if his power ran out completely, halfway to where he was going? Wherever that was.

He looked up the hill behind him, to that point his internal compass told him was west. It was steepest toward the top, and he didn't think his power reserves would carry him that far. Still, the view might help give him an idea of the wider landscape. He decided it was worth the risk.

As he turned, he looked down. Near his left foot, just touching the steel tip of his toe was a tiny green fleck.

It glistered.

Against the invasive orange of the ambient light, its green was striking. Without thinking EDDIE bent down and picked it up. It shone out brightly, reacting to his touch. As it did, he felt the valves in his chest throb. Somehow the valves absorbed the glow. He cast around him for a larger piece of gemstone. Not far away, a little further up the hill, a piece the size of a grape was lying nestled in the yellowish grass.

He picked it up.

His valves throbbed again, and he felt his strength returning.

What was going on? The simple act of picking up a gemstone shouldn't impact at all on his power reserves. Yet it did. And he was thankful for it. Being transported to where he was, may somehow have changed his atomic structure. Was that possible? Had it made him *different*? He wondered. There were more pressing, immediate questions. He put that amazing thought to one side, there would be time enough later to analyse what had happened.

Everything felt strange, wrong. His senses told him there was a difference in the gravity. The atmosphere was not the same as home, there was less oxygen. He made his way up the hill, still uncertain of his legs and how well they worked.

Had EDDIE been human he might, he supposed, be out of breath by the time he reached the top. The lower levels of oxygen would have made the climb a real battle for him. He had to pick his way carefully through the rocks that were scattered across the hillside, stopping frequently to re-map his path up to the level ground at the top. Eventually he made it to the plateau, and he turned to scan the landscape that rolled away before him, a vast yellowish-green carpet that gave way to dense brownish-tinged forest that spread out to the horizon south and east. Behind him, to the west, the hill rose to form an escarpment, a massive rock wall that towered above him.

To the north the forest thinned to yellowish-green hills. Lifting themselves up from flatter ground in the middle distance, EDDIE could make out colonnades and peristyles that might once have been parts of buildings. Further on he could see spires of dark stone that reached up toward the glowering sky. Everything felt empty. The last thing EDDIE expected to find in such a place were signs of civilization. Yet, although he could see the remains of it, he still doubted it was real. For a moment he wasn't sure he was processing the data correctly. Or maybe he lacked the deeper parameters he needed to make sense of this new information?

The wind was old and stale as if it had blown from somewhere lifeless. EDDIE couldn't hear any birds, and there was nothing in the sky but clouds.

"Is this whole world dead?" EDDIE wondered, desperately wishing he could go home.

Still, hope of returning home would not be found in these deserted wilds. The people who had made the columns and the spires and had planted the gardens, could help him get back to Crafty and Mrs McKenzie. He scanned the terrain ahead and quickly mapped the best path to the distant city and set off.

As he walked, he began daydreaming. In the background, his pathfinder subroutine kept him on track, while the unoccupied parts of his processing array found different things to think about. *"If only there was a faster way,"* he thought. And *"My legs really are rather short and are not up to long distance travel."*

This evidence suggested that Crafty had not designed him for marathons. Most likely EDDIE was designed to travel by backpack.

"If I had someone to talk to." He grumbled. *"If Crafty were here."* He wished the old radio set was linked from wherever here might be, across the vastness that he felt separated them, then he could hear Crafty's voice.

Eventually, the grass gave way to a road paved with ancient stones that were still neat and clean and level. They clicked under his metal heels, sometimes raising stark white sparks as he walked. He could see definite signs of civilization ahead, build-ings and parks and gardens, and he reasoned that someone had built them, and that it might be the same someone who had made the road.

"Were they still here?" he mused. What if they didn't want to help him? What if they were unfriendly, or downright hostile?

What if EDDIE found nothing at all, and he was stuck in this strange place forever? That last thought brought back the un-pleasant ache in his valves. He set his resolve. Whatever he did, he had to explore and exhaust every option. He would not give up. No matter what.

As he drew closer to the ruins, he could see they weren't ruins at all. The colonnades and surrounding stonework were new, and almost shiny in the thin orange sunlight. *"Who has been maintaining all this grand emptiness?"* he wondered.

The row of colonnades finally ended, and EDDIE found him-self inside a large courtyard. Between evenly spaced, low stone benches were what looked like bird baths, or fountains. He could find nothing similar in his database. Green water was dribbling down the bases of the fountains, and pooling on the stone blocks of the floor. It was as if someone had turned the tap almost off, leaving just a small trickle of water flowing.

At the exact centre of the courtyard was a single massive green geyser, surging up out of what appeared to be a crack in the stone paving. EDDIE watched in fascination as it rose and fell, sending deep green droplets scattering across the ground. These droplets bounced, clinked, and rolled until they lay still, not fluid like water, but more like crystal. EDDIE realized they were the same as the power gems he had found on the hillside. Puzzled but curious, he approached the fountain. He didn't want to get too close until he was sure that whatever it was wouldn't hurt him.

As he came near, he could hear a faint whispering, like the touch of a breath on the edges of his hearing. He did his best to tune his receptors to amplify the sound, but it eluded him. After a long moment straining to hear, he suspected he could make out words. They were strange words, alien words, words that might have been a question lingering in the still air.

EDDIE had drawn a little closer than he intended, and a glistening tendril lanced out from the fountain. EDDIE braced himself for a hard impact, instead the tip of the tendril touched him softly on the side of his head. There was the sound of a gong. It was not loud, and it faded quickly to silence, so quickly that it might not have happened at all. There was a pleasant tingling deep in his diodes and he felt one of his valves shiver.

"I wish my valves wouldn't do that," he thought absently. Something inside him shifted, as if re-calibrating.

From far away he registered a voice.

Chapter 9

The realisation came slowly that the voice EDDIE could hear was coming from the fountain in front of him.

"...Our speech will seem strange to you for ... a time ... a while ... a passing ... until you grow used to the way we speak."

The voice drifted in and out as the jets of water before him lifted and fell.

"Your speech also is strange to us," it said.

The geyser hummed and pulsated. Was it a living thing, EDDIE wondered?

"You are far from where you should be ... where you belong ... where you were made," it said. The voice sounded as if it had seeped in through the side of EDDIE's head, and dispersed like water, trickling down into his chest.

"Yes," EDDIE said, not knowing how, but sure this creature could understand him. "I really want to get home."

"Home?" the fountain whispered, as if it found the concept of the word difficult and strange, as though it understood but could not grasp its elusive meaning.

"Do you not know what home is?" EDDIE asked. "Don't you have a home?" *Everyone knew what home was, didn't they?*

There was something about the creature EDDIE liked, but he sensed he needed to be careful. There was no hostility here,

EDDIE was sure, but this was an alien, and you could never tell with aliens.

Eventually the creature broke its silence. "You are not home," it said. "Home. Being ... somewhere ... familiar ... comfortable ... pleasant ... here."

EDDIE wasn't sure he fully understood what the creature meant. If he had more experience with such things as aliens he might have felt more at ease, but his knowledge was limited. As far as he was aware, home wasn't a place that was familiar, comfortable, and pleasant, home was where you belonged and where you were loved. He found an image of Crafty and Mrs McKenzie in his memory banks. They were the only people he knew. Looking at them with his inside eye made him feel that ache at the base of his valves that he was coming to associate with strong feelings. "Does a robot have feelings?" He wondered. "Should I be worried? Maybe I am malfunctioning? Or maybe that's what makes me special?"

"Being ...us," the creature said, "We are here ... in time ... now. Yes. Also, before you came, and after, when you are not here again."

"Excuse me sir," EDDIE began as politely as he knew how. "Erm, what do I call you? Do you have a name?"

"We are Custodian," it told him, its voice louder than before. It rippled from its base upward until it pushed out a plume of deep emerald that drifted like mist, dissolving into the quiet afternoon; a soft burp that melted into a sigh.

"Please sir, I need to find my way home. Can you help?" EDDIE asked a second time.

"We could help," Custodian said. "If we were complete ... active ... fully functional."

EDDIE swivelled his head, trying to look at Custodian directly. This was hard to do as it kept slipping and flowing in and out of shape, losing its form and then finding itself again.

"I need some sort of transponder, to pick up a signal and amplify it, and to connect me with my home." EDDIE felt he wasn't making much sense. He hoped Custodian understood.

"There are many things here that might help. Come, let us look ... view ... peruse ... Archive."

Custodian began to move, somehow detaching itself from the nozzle that was projecting it. It flowed down long avenues of columns and lawns, and garden beds. As they progressed the gardens became messier. Eventually things looked totally untended, as if neatness had lost its enthusiasm.

"What is Archive?" EDDIE asked as they walked if you could describe Custodian's movement as walking. It would flow and stop, and EDDIE would wait expectantly, wondering if it were about to speak, or to point out some detail to him, but then it moved on again.

EDDIE began to picture a vast warehouse full to the roof with technologies familiar and not familiar, some totally unknown, shelving bays disappearing into the murky, hazy, indistinct distance.

Custodian stopped. It wavered and wobbled and waned and waxed as if blown backwards and forwards by some unfelt breeze. A tendril extruded and directed EDDIE's gaze toward a field of hundreds, perhaps thousands of water-like jets, each plumed at the top, each supporting a globe or cluster of globes, all of them dancing and glinting as they rose and fell.

"Here, is Archive." Custodian indicated with a tendril. "Archive is in disrepair … dysfunction … decay. We are not in full flow."

EDDIE barely registered Custodian's words. There was so much here! *How will I find what I need amongst all this?* EDDIE felt a sudden twinge of despair.

"Assist with restoration … repair … renewal … cure … healing." Custodian said.

"But," EDDIE said despondently, "I don't know how!"

"Restore Archive," Custodian said, "Gain the understanding … wisdom … knowledge … you need to return home."

EDDIE scanned the array of fountains. Where would he even start? He had no inkling at all what these things were, let alone what ailed them. "*If only I knew what the problem was*," he said to himself. He looked to Custodian for a clue, a revelation that would set him on the path to knowing what needed to be done, but Custodian remained silent.

Looking around him, EDDIE could see that some of the fountains barely flowed. This seemed to confirm that something was blocking their source. "If it's like water," EDDIE mused, "Perhaps I just need to find and fix the pipes."

Custodian lurched and began to move, but he was not going along the path that led into the field of jets that was Archive, but in the opposite direction. Here the garden was completely wild, more like a forest with trees towering above a mix of scraggly, scrappy undergrowth and unkempt wildflowers, and vines tangled up the sides of columns that once supported roofs.

Custodian's pace remained jerky and uneven. At times EDDIE had to run hard to keep up, and at other times he had to slow down to the point of making almost no forward progress at all.

"Difficult," Custodian said during one pause, as if this explained everything.

"Where are we going?" EDDIE asked, as if there were somewhere else, he could be rather than here. If Custodian told him, EDDIE wouldn't have known much more than he did now. After all, he had no reference points to work with in this strange and alien place, no map to look at, no GPS.

"Not far," Custodian said, "Not far ... a small distance ... close by."

EDDIE's suspected that they were following an old and now overgrown path. His suspicion was confirmed when the forest gave way, as if suddenly stepping back to make room for a clearing at the heart of which was a raised platform.

Custodian was perfectly still. EDDIE sensed something was about to happen.

There was the sound like air bubbles underwater and the centre of the platform started to turn, rotating anti-clockwise. As it turned it began to lift. Rising up from the cold stone was a hemisphere of shimmering green, and inside it was a shape, perfectly square and completely featureless.

"Here," said Custodian.

The grass had thinned out enough for the path to peek through. The path led straight and true to the front of the platform. Hardly had EDDIE taken this in when Custodian surged forward finding an unexpected burst of energy, a hint of its old self.

"Come. Come," it beckoned EDDIE, and surged forward, coming to a halt, almost touching the stonework of the platform.

Custodian mustered its strength and projected a tendril toward the gleaming dome. Droplets fell from the tendril, bouncing on the path and the grass, solidifying into crystals, like many emeralds, glistening in the muted forest light. After an age the tendril caressed the surface of the dome, which peeled away, like a slice of lime, opening a way to the featureless dark metal of the cube.

EDDIE felt a soft puff of air as a part of the cube melted to nothing, and EDDIE peered into a shadowy cubicle.

"There," Custodian pointed.

EDDIE felt a deep disquiet at the base of his valves. He wasn't sure he liked this at all. He hesitated, mulling it over. Is this a trap, he wondered? There was no hint that Custodian meant him any harm. The creature clearly wanted EDDIE's help.

"Fine," EDDIE said, coming to a decision: good or bad, he'd find out.

He stepped into the cubicle, and the wall reappeared silently behind him. Faint light began to seep in around him, it was faded, and its voltage was low. The floor beneath him shuddered, and the cubicle began to descend, not smoothly at first, but it seemed to get the idea as it went down.

A very long way down.

Just as EDDIE began to wonder if there was to be an end to this journey, or if the minutes would become hours and the hours days, the cubicle descent began to slow. It had finally decided that it might be a good idea after all, to come to a stop which it did with a soft, self-satisfied thud.

Chapter 10

When the door slid open, EDDIE was facing an endless, poorly lit corridor.

"Well, I can't stand here forever," EDDIE said, trying to muster his courage. In front of him part of the floor was made up of a flat metal grate with handrails on either side. He stepped forward, half expecting the door behind him to shimmer back into place, but it didn't. It stayed open, which was comforting in a way. If he decided to EDDIE would turn, step back into the elevator, and return to the surface. But if he did that, how would he ever get home? If there was any chance at all, Custodian seemed to think it was down here, at the end of this long and gloomy tunnel.

A preliminary scan revealed nothing, except a thin smear of phosphorescence on the left-hand rail. EDDIE attempted to analyse it, but its composition eluded him. It might have been that someone or something had touched the handrail and left a residue, or was it part of the rail itself? With a higher resolution scan EDDIE could see microscopic bubbles of potential energy floating, chasing each other, waiting to be directed so that they became part of an unknown circuit.

Tentatively he reached out. He was about to touch the handrail when he felt the energy focus, and a moment later the platform began to glide forward. EDDIE snatched his hand away from the rail in surprise. The platform slowed its movement. *Eureka*, he thought, which was a strange thing to think. *The proximity of my hand completes the circuit.*

Determining quickly that there wasn't enough voltage to disrupt the operation of his systems, EDDIE rested his hand on the rail and waited to see where the platform would take him.

It wasn't long before the complexion of the corridor changed. The light grew steadily dimmer and small patches of decay became evident. There were broken tiles, and water dripped from poorly maintained pipes. The walls were covered in some greyish membrane. And then there was the smell; heavy, musty, and cloying. If he had a stomach EDDIE knew it would be dancing a jig. Even without a stomach, he had to dampen his sensors, dialling down their sensitivity. The place smelled and felt like animals. Looking around, EDDIE couldn't tell if anything other than slime and bacteria still lived here. The platform slowed down. It was making heavy weather of moving through the goop that had pooled across its tracks, gumming up whatever mechanism it used.

The goop thickened the further he went, until the platform came to a sticky, viscous halt.

"Now what?"

He peered ahead into thickening darkness. The way was forward, but the thought of climbing down and proceeding on foot made him feel queasy. That muck had been sitting on the floor of the tunnel for goodness knew how long. EDDIE was positive there were things living in it, waiting for an unsuspecting little robot to wade past. They were ready, itching to latch onto him and suck every joule of energy from his electronic veins, leaving him crumpled like an old tin can, rusting in the ooze.

EDDIE shuddered. "Yech," he said with an emphatic clack of all his relays. "They've really let this place go."

"You don't know the half of it," a voice sounded from somewhere overhead.

"Who said that?" EDDIE asked, realizing how dumb that sounded.

"Well, I did, of course."

"Yes, I got that bit," EDDIE said, "But who are you?"

"I am Vosna." The voice was light, and gentle. It was melodious, feminine, and without accent. "Engineer, Second Class. At your service."

EDDIE felt the glow of pride she had in her title. It meant something to her; she must have worked hard to earn it.

"Who or perhaps what are you, strange visitor?" The voice that called itself Vosna inquired.

"EDDIE," said EDDIE. What more could he say. He was and as far as he knew, always would be EDDIE. "Yes," he added, confirming it. "I am EDDIE."

"What's an EDDIE?" Vosna inquired, sounding curious.

"An EDDIE is me," EDDIE said. This of course should have explained everything, at least EDDIE thought so. It should have been obvious to someone who was smart enough to call themselves an Engineer, Second Class.

"You are clearly some variety of machine?"

"Yes, of course."

"But what type of machine?"

"I am an Electronic Data Digester and Inference Engine," EDDIE said. "EDDIE. No gaps, no full stops, it's a name not just an acronym."

"I see," Vosna said. "I perceive you to be a very fine machine indeed."

"Thank you," EDDIE was starting to like whoever it was who owned the voice. "But I am much more than just a machine."

"Of course," said Vosna, Engineer, Second Class. "But they all say that."

"Do they?" EDDIE wondered how many robots like him she had met that had made such a claim. If Vosna was old, she might have met who-knew-how-many machines of different types. The older you are, the more likely it is that you have met all sorts of different kinds of people, EDDIE supposed. Some would be nice. Some not so nice. Some would be real criminals, nasty to their core. He didn't like the sound of meeting anyone like that. There was something to be said for kindness. People had nice things to say about you when you were kind to them.

It occurred to EDDIE that he could try to be a little kinder to Vosna, though she was being a bit nosy. She was being cautious in her curiosity, or curious in her cautiousness. After all, how would she know that *he* wasn't some criminal mastermind, or an alien hostile, or something much worse? Whatever that might be.

"My pressing question," Vosna interrupted EDDIE's thoughts, "Is where did you come from, and what do you want? What has brought you all the way down here, to me?"

EDDIE was trying to work out how to answer that question, when she spoke again: "You're certainly not one of those *other* things, which makes you something else entirely."

"It seems that way," EDDIE said. It was obvious. At least to him. "I am definitely not one of those other '*things*,' whatever they are. I am EDDIE."

"Yes, you said," Vosna agreed. "But I must be careful. I can't take everyone at face value. That would get me into all sorts of trouble. There is a line of accountability, don't you know? Yes, there is. That's for sure."

EDDIE couldn't argue with her logic, although he did wonder what a line of accountability was. It was probable that there was someone who went by the title of Engineer, First Class and that made them sound important. EDDIE felt sure that an Engineer, First class would want an Engineer, Second Class to be cautious about these things. EDDIE wondered how you spoke to someone who was that important? For someone as important as that wouldn't you have to make an appointment?

Was Custodian important? EDDIE was sure he was, but he didn't have much evidence to answer that question.

"Well," EDDIE began, "I was helping someone who said they might be able to find a way for me to get home."

"Someone?" Vosna pressed. "Who was it?"

"Up on the surface," EDDIE explained. He wasn't filling in many of the gaps, that's for sure. "There really isn't much to tell."

"You came from the *surface*?" Vosna asked in a reverent whisper.

"Is that a good thing or a bad thing?" EDDIE asked, wondering if he'd made some mistake.

"The surface is still there?"

"Yes, of course. That's where I came from."

"I didn't dare to hope," Vosna said. "I suspected that's where they came from. If they were from the surface ... But I thought it no longer existed, at least not in the way I remembered it. Not in a good way. Once the flow stopped, surely everything died? Everything stopped working down here. I haven't been able to do my job. I haven't been able to maintain the systems assigned to me. I wonder, all the time, what has gone wrong. And now, here you are, telling me that you have come from the surface. So I must ask: How can you have come from the surface! How could they be from the surface?"

"I don't know. I'm sorry. I haven't been here very long. I mean, I only arrived today," EDDIE said, hoping to mollify Vosna. "But I can assure you that the surface is very much there. I saw some ruined buildings and lots of overgrown gardens. If that's of any help?"

"They arrived some time ago. I have never seen their like before. They are a new species perhaps? Maybe like you they are from somewhere else, from somewhere far away. Are you hunting them? Or are you *on their side*?"

"If I knew who they were, I might be able to answer your questions," EDDIE said. "I am just here to help Custodian."

"Ooooh," Vosna said, half exhalation, half exclamation, completely in awe. "*Custodian* is it?"

"Custodian needs to reactivate Archive. If I can help him to do that, then he might help me get home; back to Crafty, and Mrs McKenzie."

"Forgive me, EDDIE, I had to be sure," Vosna said. "You must come! You must come now!"

Before EDDIE could think, let alone respond, a shaft of light sliced through the wall of the tunnel and widened into a hatchway. Something loomed in the light. EDDIE could not make out what it was, only that it was a silhouette of an indistinct shape.

"Come," Vosna said, her voice somehow close to EDDIE's aural receptors. "Don't delay. Time is short."

EDDIE gingerly clambered down from the platform, fearing his feet would be covered in goop, but where the light had spilled across the tunnel's floor the caustic slime had shrunk away revealing cold clean steel.

EDDIE stepped through the hatch, and the doorway closed tightly behind him.

Chapter 11

E DDIE found himself, not in a cramped crawl space as he had been expecting, but a comfortable corridor that was well lit and clean.

Directly in front of him, floating like an amber bubble, or a football sized raindrop caught in a sunset was …

"Vosna! Yes, this is me. Welcome EDDIE, come, come, I will show you many things for your understanding, and for your assistance. Perhaps I too can help you in your quest to return home?"

With some trepidation, EDDIE followed the Engineer, Second Class as she bobbed her way down the corridor like a cork on the ocean.

"This is it!" Vosna stopped. "This is where I spend most of my time." Another hatchway slipped open, and they went through into a hemispherical room.

In the exact centre was what appeared to be a white bowl that floated above the floor. It was to this that Vosna bobbled. She rose slightly, and moved forwards, settling into the bowl with a quiet, happy sigh. The amber of her skin rippled softly as if in satisfaction, and for a few moments she was very still.

Without warning a dark blue line split the wall in half horizontally. It expanded up and down and formed a band, a ribbon that separated floor from ceiling. Slowly, like an old television warming up, panel-like images began to appear. They were hazy at first, but they steadily became sharp and clear.

EDDIE looked at the first image that became recognisable. This viewing panel started to flip between static images of maintenance corridors. EDDIE wasn't interested in those, but he supposed it was important to whoever kept an eye on the smooth running of this strange place to see them.

On the second viewing panel EDDIE could make out a vast cavernous space that had possibly been carved out of rock by long ages of flowing water. He could see where a small lake had been dammed. He could see a pipeline intended to divert the natural flow of the water that had been there in the past. There were three maintenance lamps fixed to the rock wall either side and above the massive pipes that jutted from the rock in the far distance. The pipes were almost dry: a bare dribble of water was falling into what was left of the reservoir.

EDDIE's task seemed clear: to revive Custodian and to restore Archive he had to restore full flow through the pipes. From what he had seen on the surface, EDDIE knew that the city was dying of thirst. To understand it, EDDIE had to see it, and seeing it, EDDIE had trouble coming to terms with it: the problem at the least, was the vast, incredible, mind-numbing scale of everything. He was only a little robot after all. In the scheme of the things he was seeing, he felt so much smaller.

Vosna manipulated the image that EDDIE was looking at, and the picture narrowed in on part of the lake itself. EDDIE knew that it was nowhere near its former grandeur. From this angle it was little more than a shallow pool of phosphorescent liquid. He wondered briefly at the phosphorescence. It was part of the water down here, but he hadn't seen it on the surface.

Vosna moved slightly in her seat, and the onscreen image changed. EDDIE saw that the pool was much larger than he first thought. It was not a pool at all but an enormous dam that stretched to the limit of the cameras and past the edges of the light. It vanished into the unknown black.

Not only had the pipes dried to a trickle, but the dam wall was dry. Though the lake was vast, the water levels were painfully low; clearly, nothing had flowed over the spillway for the longest age. That meant nothing was flowing through to give life to the city above.

"Here!" Vosna said. "This is what I wanted you to see."

A third panel had resolved to clarity. Vosna had extruded an amber tendril and was using this to point at the image. There was a sudden blur of motion. Something was on the lake shore. Something the camera couldn't pick up clearly. It was too quick for the cameras' capacity to focus. Something was agitating the water, splashing in the shallows.

EDDIE turned away from the video panels. He was about to ask Vosna if she was able to do something with the clarity of the picture.

"Please EDDIE," she implored him. "Just wait and watch. You will see. You will see!"

EDDIE turned his attention back to the screen. The phosphorescent surface seethed and then settled, roiled, then became still. As he watched something came up out of the lake, flippy-flopping its happy way onto the stony shore.

"It's the Muk'Vuh!"

And then, following it out of the water came another. And another.

Four and five.

Seven.

Twelve.

More, until the beach was fairly crammed with flipping and flopping, and though EDDIE couldn't hear it, he knew there was a cacophony of their thick phlegmy banter. In the muted colour of the video panel EDDIE saw differences between the creatures. Some were crested with spines, yellow and blue and deep red; some had small crests, others were much larger. "*Was it dependent on their age?*" EDDIE mused. Their bodies were all shades of glistening green and grey and lumpy brown.

"Oh ..." EDDIE blipped.

And the largest one, had a crest of beetroot red, tipped with burnt orange. Even in the gloaming, this Muk'Vuh stood out. Even from here EDDIE could sense his authority. He must be their leader. EDDIE needed a clearer view to be sure, but he knew this Muk'Vuh.

"Yes," Vosna agreed. "Very sincerely 'Oh!'"

"They have made themselves at home, haven't they?"

"Yes. They came from upstream. Just after the noise, but that was a long time after the flow had stopped. How long I don't know, I can't even guess. Our chronometers stopped working. Who knows why?"

Vosna shifted where she sat. "I don't know how they found their way in. They didn't come through the pipes. These cameras aren't recorded, nothing is, not since the flow stopped, so I can't search back to discover how they arrived. I don't suppose it matters much. They are here now."

On screen, several of the larger Muk'Vuh had moved away from the main group. They gathered around the one with the beetroot red crest and the fiery orange tips.

"Is there audio?" EDDIE asked hopefully.

"No, not from there," Vosna said. "And even if there were, voice emulation hasn't been successful translating their way of speech. I have been trying since they first arrived."

EDDIE remembered the tingle of Custodian's touch and the understanding that followed. Custodian had installed the ability for EDDIE to translate language.

"That one in the middle," Vosna said. "The biggest one. He is the one who sometimes goes exploring. If you had stayed on the transport, your path would have taken you to the maintenance pods you can see there to the left."

EDDIE would have come face to face, not with one Muk'Vuh but the whole tribe, and he didn't want to think how that might have ended. His innards shuddered. "I am glad that didn't happen. And I have met that big one before and I can tell you, he has a real attitude problem."

Vosna was silent for a long time. If she was looking at the screen, EDDIE couldn't tell. She started to speak. "Early today, several of the bigger ones, the males, left the mothers and infants. They worked out how to open the pod doors, and they travelled together, down to the access tunnel, as far as the transport tube. But they refused to go any further. They stood there for the longest time. This is when I recorded their language for analysis.

"I am positive they were arguing about what to do next. They left the big one behind near the access way and returned to the lake. But the big one, he is brave, and he is smart. He rode the transport to the end. Once he arrived there, he worked out how to use the elevator and he went up all the way to the city."

EDDIE wondered about the beetroot coloured Muk'Vuh's motivation. "Perhaps if he could find a safe way out, he might convince the others to follow?"

"To where?"

"I have no idea," EDDIE replied, picturing Crafty and Mrs McKenzie. "Perhaps, like me, he wants to go home."

"Home?" Vosna sounded it out slowly, as if unfamiliar with the word and the concept.

"You know. It's the place you belong the most," EDDIE said. As he said it, he felt that now familiar ache ripple across his relays. "That must have been when he somehow found his way into Crafty's carrier beam and to us!"

"But not home?"

"No, not home," EDDIE sighed. "Well, not his home. Not the home he was hoping to find. And now, no thanks to him, I too am very far from home."

"They are in a place that is strange to them," Vosna mused. She rippled where she sat. She didn't seem to grasp this idea of "home." It seemed to EDDIE she was reacting to his display of emotion. It was new to him, being able to feel the way he suspected people felt. He didn't know how to apply it. His experience was so limited. He was sure there were other ways to react to things than feeling sad, or uncertain. He had locked onto the importance of home. He knew it was a place that was safe, except for the occasional visit from wayward Muk'Vuh, which he hoped was something that didn't happen too often. He knew that home was a place he could learn and grow. It's where he was supposed to be. He wondered if this is how the Muk'Vuh felt about the home he had left?

"Noise," EDDIE said suddenly and loud enough to startle Vosna, which wasn't an easy feat with the tiny sound bar Crafty had installed. EDDIE was thankful that at least Crafty configured stereo.

"Noise?"

"Yes. You said something before. You said they came downstream, after the noise, after the flow had stopped. What noise?"

"Yes! They did. But it was long after the flow stopped. I think. The flow hasn't been there for a very long time." Vosna appeared deep in thought. "It was a very big noise. There was a frightening vibration. The lights flickered. Many of the routines stalled. Some things came back online. But not many. Mostly everything is still down. Almost nothing is working." There was sadness in Vosna's voice. It was hard for her to admit how bad things were.

"When did this happen?" EDDIE asked. He wasn't sure why it was important. Something in the back of his processors niggled him. If he could firm up the timeline in his head, he would know if the noise and the end of flow were connected. It was a puzzle, and he was made to solve puzzles. But he needed all the pieces.

"I could not tell you how long. More than minutes. More than days. Perhaps weeks or months. I do not know. There is no way for me to calibrate time." She made a sound like a sigh. "I know this is something Engineers should know. I feel they should, but I do not," Vosna replied.

"And things are still offline?" EDDIE asked.

"Everything major is offline, now that the flow has stopped." Vosna's confirmed.

EDDIE wasn't sure what came first; the flow stopping, and the routines shutting down as a result. Or had it been the other way around? And did it matter when it came to getting things running again.

"It has been offline for a long time, judging by what I saw on the surface." EDDIE observed.

"Please, EDDIE, if you can, you must help," she said, but her uncertainty was plain. "Can you help?"

"I don't know," EDDIE told her. "I will try. I need to try."

EDDIE sensed her relief.

"But ..." he said.

She looked at him expectantly. At least he thought she did. She didn't have any eyes that were obvious to him.

"If I am to do anything," he said, "I *will* need your help."

"Anything," Vosna whispered. Her amber skin flamed in patches, orange with excitement. "Yes, anything I can do, I will help. We will fix this together."

Chapter 12

I f only I could speak to Crafty. He'd know what to do.

"*Follow logic's path to the truth,*" a voice said. It was almost Crafty's, but not quite. EDDIE decided it was more like an echo or a memory, which made him wonder: "*Do I remember things that happened before I was turned on? Is that possible?*"

Was there a hint of another time flavouring his boot sector? Did it load itself into his neural network the moment he came to life? EDDIE doubted machines had memories. But then, he suspected he was no ordinary machine. After all it was Crafty's idea to create a little robot that was unique; a little robot who did and computed things differently. Crafty had made EDDIE special.

For whatever lay ahead, EDDIE knew, he would need every bit of special that Crafty had built into him. "Is there another way to the surface?" EDDIE asked. "Other than the way I came in?"

"Oh, yes," Vosna replied. "Many ways have been put in place. There are many access points for maintenance."

Vosna detached herself from the cradle and bobbed toward the hatchway, which had opened ahead of her. "Come, EDDIE," she said. "Follow, and you will see."

Once again EDDIE and Vosna were standing in the corridor. It curved away before them, wrapping itself around the shape of the control room. Vosna drifted forward, leading the way. They passed into a tangled maze of tunnels and rooms, sometimes switching back as they angled around equipment, to return once again to their original heading. EDDIE did his best to calibrate his pathfinder, but the best he could do was conclude that they were heading away from the city.

He had no idea where they were going, or what they would do when they got there. Having a proper context to work with is vital when you need to solve a puzzle. *That's why it's good to know where* here *is*, EDDIE thought. Despite his feelings of doubt, EDDIE knew he had to trust Vosna. As with Custodian, EDDIE sensed no hint of hostility whatever. She was eager for EDDIE's help. EDDIE was certain the disappearance of First Engineer would have left her floundering around, not knowing what to do with those processes she hadn't been shown how to manage. *You have to learn the basics first, after all, and you can't learn them on your own.* He knew how she felt. Vosna was missing First Engineer the same way he was missing Crafty.

In EDDIE she had a glimmer of hope. Together they might be able to set things right. Vosna was compelled to do what she had been training for, whatever the gaps in her knowledge might be, and she seemed to be the only one here. The least EDDIE could do was to keep up his air of confidence, even if confidence was the last thing he felt.

"I'll wing it," EDDIE decided, but that didn't make him feel any better. He wasn't sure what "winging it" meant. He assumed it was like flying by the seat of your pants, although he didn't know what that meant either. There was one thing for sure, because robots don't need to wear pants, and they certainly don't have wings, they *weren't* meant to fly.

As they made their way along yet another boring and odourless corridor, it occurred to EDDIE that that's what the "Inference" part of his name meant. He was EDDIE, the *Inference* engine. *Give me the data and I'll figure it out.* Solving puzzles was what he did. He could work with that, except now he didn't have much of anything to work with, and for some reason that made him glum, and he didn't want to be glum; glum wouldn't help him to achieve anything.

They came around a sharp right-hand corner and their corridor opened out into some kind of terminus. EDDIE stopped and gazed around. He and Vosna were standing on a wide platform covered in white, black, blue, and green mosaic tiles that swirled around in dizzying patterns. Directly to his right was a row of elevator doors. They were all shut tight, their buttons glowing white, waiting for someone to press them.

To their left were six transporter tracks with raised platforms in between. He noted the grime on the tiles, and the dirt and rubbish that was swirling around in the transport pits. Once, this place would have been bustling with activity, but now it was abandoned to disuse and emptiness.

Vosna had gone ahead and had stopped in front of the last elevator. EDDIE didn't see her extend a tendril to press the button, but the elevator door slid open with a soft swoosh.

"Please EDDIE," she said. "This is the one you must use."

EDDIE hesitated in front of the open door. He was expecting Vosna to come with him, and he gave her a quizzical look.

"No, EDDIE, I cannot go with you. I am tethered to the maintenance areas and to the control room. This is as far as I am able to go."

EDDIE wanted to nod, but his head wouldn't let him, and he felt the ability to shrug might have been useful. When he got home, he would try and convince Crafty to make the appropriate modifications.

When he got home...

But first, there were things to do.

He stepped into the elevator with a stronger sense of resolve. He lifted a hand and gave a little wave to reassure Vosna that everything would work out fine.

The door closed in an instant and EDDIE felt himself rising.

Chapter 13

E DDIE emerged into muted afternoon sunlight in the middle of a forest that was utterly silent.

To be outside in the open air, with the sky overhead, completely free of corridors, brought about a different, bigger, excited feeling that drenched his circuits. It took EDDIE a while to notice that even here, away from the city, nothing was moving in the thick undergrowth. Nothing was moving in the trees above his head. Nothing was flying or chirruping or squawking or buzzing. It was as if the whole world lacked the energy to muster the breath required to stir the smallest twig.

Do they have seasons here if there was no wind to carry them? EDDIE wondered. *If the wind blew more than it did, the sky might not be so orange, carrying around its burden of old dust that was never settled by falling rain.* He leaned back to look up. *Would Vosna change colour if the sky changed? If she were on earth, would she go from amber to marble blue?*

Where had that thought come from?

"Ahh, I'm inferring again!" EDDIE said to himself. Thoughts are strange things. To a robot they should be nothing more than bits of data. But EDDIE found himself taking those bits of data, and examining them and putting them together, linking them in patterns that made sense and that he could draw conclusions

from. He wondered if that's what humans did; would doing the same thing mean that he was a little bit human?

The door completely closed as soon as EDDIE stepped out of the elevator. Was that meant to make him feel he was shut out forever, or was it urging him forward? Was he now trapped in a different but still unknown space, or was he being challenged to explore, to go deeper into this world that wasn't his? He couldn't go back, so forward was his only option.

He decided that there were lots of qualities a good explorer should have. He should crave adventure and love taking risks. That meant being brave, even if you didn't feel brave at the time. In forests like these adventurers met cannibals. So far EDDIE hadn't met any real-life cannibals. He hadn't met much of anything. Besides, EDDIE was sure that a real-life cannibal wasn't going to catch and cook up a little robot, unless they mistook him for a can of beans.

EDDIE hadn't met any real-life explorers either, but he couldn't let that stop him. Real life explorers would be bold and brave and forward-looking, curious, and tenacious. He knew he needed to be all those things if he was going to head out deeper into the unknown. *It's mine to make real. Mine to claim and conquer, to raise the flag and make a speech. After all, that's what real explorers did.*

"Of course, I can't stay here. I need to move on." EDDIE concluded, suddenly feeling much better about things.

The flow of everything that was important in this place had slowed down. Eventually it would grind to a complete stop. A trickle through long dry pipes was better than the alternative. If everything turned to thirsty dust, then everything he had seen so far would shrivel up and die. Custodian would cease to be, no longer a fountain plume, but an insipid puddle.

EDDIE felt a great sense of urgency hit him. *"Why am I feeling sorry for myself?"* He wondered. *"I'm letting homesickness get the better of me. There was no way I am going to drop the ball. Not a chance. That's not the kind of robot I am."*

Doing the right thing is sometimes the hardest thing you can do, he realised.

As if from a vast distance he heard Mrs McKenzie's voice: "Oh for goodness sake, stop faffing around would you?! You are overthinking everything. Just get on with it!"

He did not have the physical capacity to smile, instead he made a little noise that seemed to him to be a happy noise.

"Sometimes faffing is necessary," EDDIE informed the distant Mrs McKenzie, "And ... *and* if not necessary then unavoidable. And to infer, to truly be an inference engine, you must take time to consider all the possibilities. Which is, categorically not in any way shape or form, faffing!" He doubted he had the ability to convince Mrs McKenzie that this was a cold hard indisputable fact; he was sure she'd have something definite and robust to say in response and in the end, he'd lose the argument.

Having bolstered himself with thoughts of home, he set a scan running, to probe as deep into the forest as it would go; although the scan seemed reluctant to wander too far. If the scans didn't find anything, then EDDIE didn't have to worry. Or did he? It meant that the scan hadn't found anything it identified as threatening. The problem was this didn't make EDDIE feel secure. You never knew what was hiding around the next corner, waiting, eager, drooling, ready to chomp and chew. He'd ruled out cannibals. What else would find a little robot like him palatable, digestible, and tasty?

With that thought rattling around in his head, he quickly hobbled together a pattern for a wide area probe and triggered the routine. It wasn't long before his scans had given the landscape ahead of him definite shape. The pipes were easy to make out: side by side by side, they ran dry and lifeless from the city deeper into a forest that was struggling to hang on to whatever life it had.

The pipes, EDDIE knew, fed the underground lake. When levels were normal, the overflow would run fast through all the rivulets and streams, in torrents, and vitality would restore this thirsty land. As far as his sensors could discern the pipes were not compromised in any way. They were structurally sound. There were no breaks, that EDDIE could detect. That was a huge relief. He had no idea how he would repair them if they were damaged.

Opposite the elevator was a clearing: yet, it was not empty space, for it was filled with a building. A windowless, imposing building. It was darker than the shadows cast over it as the sun began to settle beneath the mountains off to the west. The encroaching darkness made EDDIE nervous. Quiet and lifeless as the day had seemed, EDDIE didn't know what the night would bring; nocturnal things, roaming things, hungry things.

"You're letting it get to you. You have no data to support any of it."

"Ever forwards, never backwards," EDDIE said to himself, and as quickly as his legs allowed, he crossed to where he thought he saw an oblong that was a slightly lighter shade than the metal around it. He hoped it was a door.

"If only Vosna was here," EDDIE lamented. "She'd know how to get this open."

"Oh, but I am here, EDDIE," A familiar voice sounded through the dusk. "When Custodian first met with you, and touched you, he gave you voice emulation."

"Voice *what?*"

"Emulation. It works sub-atomically. It translates, but it also allows us to speak to each other, even across a distance."

"Like radio," EDDIE said, getting it straight in his head. "I'm wired for sound?"

"It has many uses," Vosna agreed. She made a chiming sound, and EDDIE felt it was laughter. "It works underneath and through audible sound waves."

"Like Blu-Tooth?"

Vosna sighed. "If you must."

EDDIE looked around. Behind him the shadows were starting to thicken, deepening until he could no longer see the trees or the clearing. Once again, he wondered what might be lurking, using the darkness as cover. He scanned quickly but found nothing. He felt that there might be things that could evade detection, the shadows, mists, wisps that lurked at the very edge of his sensors.

"Vosna," he said, hoping his voice wasn't shaking. "I don't suppose you could open this door for me? It's getting kind of dark out here."

"Silly," said Vosna. "Of course I can."

The door slid open, slowly, shuddering on tracks that hadn't been used for a long time. EDDIE stepped into a vast, dark, and empty space.

Chapter 14

T he door juddered shut behind him and EDDIE found himself standing in utter, cave deep darkness.

"If this is what it's like to have an adventure," EDDIE said, "You can keep it all to yourself!"

"Don't be glum," Vosna said brightly, "Just turn on the lights!"

"And how do propose I do that? I can't see my hand in front of my face, let alone a light switch?"

"Oh silly little robot." Vosna laughed. "Just ask it."

"What?" For a moment EDDIE was flummoxed. "Oh! You mean ... Right. OK!"

In his firmest voice, which wasn't firm, or large, EDDIE said: "Lights On!"

There was a sudden flickering, and a soft effusive glow began to spread slowly, seeping into the deepest corners of shadow. EDDIE looked around but couldn't find the source. The light seemed to leak into the cavernous space, from everywhere. Had he been greeted with bank after reluctant bank, flickering like old fluorescent tubes he might have been more comfortable. The light gave up its efforts of finding anything close to a satisfactory brightness and settled into a kind of twilight that barely revealed anything in the gloom.

"Matches the mood I guess," EDDIE commented.

"Emergency lighting," Vosna agreed.

"It's better than nothing." EDDIE thought having some sort of light source of his own would be handy. He made a mental note to mention that one to Crafty as well.

EDDIE gazed around for a long time trying to figure out what he was seeing. From the outside it had looked like a warehouse. Inside was against all his expectations. He could have expected floor to ceiling racking, bay after bay stacked with crates and pallets, but this was different. Here all manner things were floating in the air. He could see pieces of machinery, all different sizes, and spare parts gathered in clumps like fruit in a bowl. They were evenly spaced apart, with the heavier objects closer to the floor and the smaller lighter ones above them, and still others floating up near the ceiling. If the light was brighter EDDIE might have made out some sense of order, and what kept them aloft.

There were no signs of age. There was no dust, no puddles of rain that had leaked through the roof to gather on the floor, and there were no smudges of oil where machinery had cried out its disrepair. It all looked brand new, as if it had been made and stored yesterday.

"Oh, my," EDDIE breathed. What could he infer from all this? Where would he start?

He began to weave his way through the forest of floating parts. He touched what might have been a pump. It slowly started to spin, tumbling end over end. And yet, it did not move more than a millimeter or two from its original position.

"EDDIE?"

"Yes Vosna?"

"What are you looking for? Perhaps I can help you find it?"

"To be honest, Vosna, I don't know. Inspiration maybe? I figure I'll know it when I see it," he said, trying to sound confident.

When he found what was wrong with the pipeline, he knew he'd need more than a toothpick and a teabag to fix it, and he didn't have those. "I have no idea what I'll need. A toolkit maybe, whatever stands in for tools around here. For a start, I'd settle for some way to scout that pipeline," he said, trying to herd his tumbled jumble of thoughts together. "I'd rather not walk. It'd take too long, and I don't have the inclination." He sighed. "I swear, I have legs shorter than ET."

He spotted something out of the corner of his microdot-camera eyes that stopped him cold. He swivelled his gaze towards it and zoomed in a click or two. At first, he thought it was a clump of black dust particles, but it was moving, like a swarm of midges, swirling, expanding, collapsing in on itself, to spring outward, an explosion of gyrating black dots. EDDIE edged closer, zoomed in another click or two. He reached out with a finger, hoping to catch one of the little dots unaware, so he could examine it. As if it had been wafted by a breeze he didn't feel, one of the tiny particles came to rest on his silicone fingertip. He stared down at it, cranking his gaze into full macro to come close to seeing what it was.

EDDIE made his best approximation of a happy noise. On his finger was a tiny round, four-legged robot, with a single camera-eye which was swivelled upward so it could get a better look at EDDIE.

"Grab a handful of them EDDIE," Vosna advised. "They will separate easily from the swarm. See, even now they are putting together a convention!"

A black mist, more like a smudge against his vision than any-thing else, was forming on EDDIE's outstretched hands. The lit-tle robots nestled together in the cup he made with his palms. He pulled his hands slowly away from the swarm, but none of the midge sized robots in the main body followed.

"What are they?" EDDIE asked, awestruck.

"Nanobots," Vosna said, happily. "You have your toolkit."

The fist sized swarm moved up from his hand and settled around his wrist in a black band. Once he was sure they weren't going to fall off, he continued to explore the huge warehouse. Af-ter what was a lot of walking on his short legs EDDIE came to the end of a row of floating parts and gadgets.

Ahead of him there were huge sliding doors, partly open and admitting the chill of the deepening night. He glanced to his right and felt a glow of satisfaction.

"Bingo," he said. Was it too soon to think things might be looking up? He wondered. He had started to connect the warm feeling in his bits and bytes to what might be called optimism.

"Hey Vosna?" EDDIE called. "Is that what I think it is and does it still work?"

"Insufficient information."

EDDIE took a few moments to sum up his impressions. "It looks like a vehicle," he said. In the middle of a disc was a hemispherical seat like Vosna's cradle. From each of the four main compass points protruded what EDDIE thought looked like a Chuppa Chupp: a white composite stick supporting a glistening silver sphere.

"Is anything around here made for robots my size and shape?" EDDIE wondered despondently. If comfort was an imperative, it would be a deal breaker, but the cradle was serviceable enough. He'd have to cross his legs, but that would be OK. He was a robot, so it wasn't like he'd get pins and needles from sitting in the same place for too long.

He examined the vehicle more closely in the dim glow available from the emergency lighting.

"How does this thing even work?" he wondered.

He couldn't see engines that would provide lift, and there didn't seem to be any way of steering it. For all he knew it might not be a vehicle at all, it might be this world's version of a fidget spinner. He wasn't worried though, around here nothing was ever as it seemed.

Back in the control room, he'd watched as Vosna floated into position in her cradle. To do that EDDIE had to grab hold of one of the white composite sticks and lift himself awkwardly onto the edge of the disk. From there he scooched across and settled himself as best he could in a seat designed for a very different backside.

"Hmmm." He scanned around. The cockpit had no dials, or switches, no yoke or joystick or steering wheel. There wasn't even a tiller! EDDIE was surrounded by featureless grey plastic. Was he facing forwards, and did it matter? He jiggled himself around, and as he did, his fingers brushed across the plastic. He might have imagined it, but he thought he heard a soft click. There was a change in sensation, the air was now tingling with static. Low at first, and almost inaudible to EDDIE's sensitive hearing, was a hum. It was soft, and gentle, like white noise far away. Each of the spheres had activated, and rainbow colours had started chasing each other across their surfaces.

EDDIE hadn't noticed it at first, but a sphere, the size of a tennis ball, but thin and transparent as a soap bubble, had appeared near his right hand. He lifted his hand, wanting to touch it, but fearing it might burst. It seemed to know what to do, and quickly positioned itself in his metallic palm. Although it looked fragile it was anything but. Its surface was pliable. He turned it over in his hand to examine it more closely. As he did the craft lifted gently off the ground. The white noise changed, deepening in intensity.

After some experimentation, EDDIE found that if he lifted the sphere, the craft lifted. If he lowered the sphere, the craft settled to the ground. Pushing the sphere to the right and the craft went right. Left and it went left.

With some trepidation EDDIE set off for a slow cruise around the warehouse, sticking as close as he could to the walls. He didn't want to disturb the floating inventory, or worse, hit something and wreck his ride. He quickly got the hang of how the contraption worked. Subtle changes of the position of the sphere and he could manoeuvre deftly through the forest of spare parts. As his confidence grew, he pushed up his speed.

"Way cool!"

EDDIE would never have considered himself daring, but he found himself having fun while he mastered tight turns, donuts, and best of all, drifts. He discovered that the craft had its own fail-safe's. Twice he came close to smashing into a wall, to have the machine spin away from disaster, quick as a Hamilton jet boat, a wash of ozone-tinged air pluming over him.

"*This will do,*" he thought. "*Yes, this will do very well.*"

Chapter 15

The first wash of dawn found EDDIE in sleep mode.

There were only so many donuts a little robot could spin, and he'd had more than enough of drifting and there was little else to do in a vast warehouse full of strange objects. He could have spent time analysing those gadgets that were the most interesting, finding out what they did and if any would help with his mission to fix the flow in the pipes and restore the city, but there were just too many bits and pieces, and it would take way too long for his liking.

He ran a system check or two, did a backup, and powered down. He might have dreamed, if robots dream, at least that's what he suspected they were, but he didn't know as he had never been to sleep before, and he had never had a dream. He might have dreamed of somewhere he once knew. There were faces. A boy with unkempt dark hair. A Calico cat. A black and white dog, and something else, something flippy-floppy and alien. The faces dissolved, to be replaced by endless doors, in endless hallways, and strobing red lights that made him feel jittery. He felt a creeping cold, and he wanted to find the thermostat to turn up the heat, but the thermostat kept darting out of his way and his hands were too slow. It didn't matter how hard he tried, he couldn't move fast enough, and it was so cold he couldn't feel his fingers. He knew in the dream that he was a robot. That's all he was. But he wanted to feel, to sense what he was touching. He wanted to taste and to smell. But all he could do was analyse the particles that came in contact with his sensors and infer, infer what they smelled like, infer what they tasted like. It all felt like guesswork.

Muffled and far away someone said: "You are an inference engine."

"EDDIE?"

A voice, soft, gentle, melodious, and kind.

"EDDIE?"

A quiet hum from somewhere deep in his chest.

"It's time to wake up."

The voice was familiar. He was sure it belonged to a friend.

He felt his fans spin up and his micro-dot-cameras went from cool black to a deep green. Did he have to be awake? There was something comforting in being in that holding pattern of not quite conscious.

"Five more minutes, please?"

"EDDIE!" That voice, firmer and louder.

"No fair," he said.

Bright sunlight was slamming in through the open doors, spearing him where he sat. It was still early, not long past sunrise, but he had grown accustomed to the muted lighting of the warehouse from the night before. If he had eyelids he'd have blinked. Instead, his visual processors registered bright light and increased the level of filtering. After a moment the light was less intense.

"Erg," he said. "I know, I know, thanks Vosna, time doesn't wait, not for people, not for robots. There's work to be done. And I am just the robot to do it!"

He leaped to his feet and looked around, and his heart sank. He had to navigate the little glider out the door before he could do anything. But the door wasn't open wide enough. EDDIE leaned back to look up. The door was big. EDDIE looked at the door. He turned and looked back at the glider. Then he looked back at the door. It wasn't going to fit.

"Don't think," he said to himself. *"Just do. Roll up your sleeves and get it done."*

Several minutes of grunting and pushing and straining later EDDIE had the door open wide enough to navigate the little gilder through it and into the morning light. Before he had gone into sleep mode last night, EDDIE had figured out how the vehicle was charged, and he'd plugged it in. There was no way to tell how much power the craft had stored in its batteries as the whole place was on emergency supply. He didn't know if he'd end up travelling ten meters or one hundred kilometers. He would have to take the little crafts' power reserves on faith.

He had to follow the pipeline: that much made sense. He had to find the blockage and restore the flow. He still had no clue how he would do that. EDDIE suspected that Vosna didn't know either. She knew lots about some stuff, and nothing about other stuff. Someone might accuse him of the same thing, he supposed. He was sure he'd heard someone say that wisdom came with experience and with observing other people's mistakes. *"Sounds so simple,"* EDDIE mused.

If there was something he didn't know, he would simply ask Crafty. If there was something Vosna didn't know, she could ask Engineer, First Class. Except Engineer, First class was missing. It was down to EDDIE and Vosna and what they knew. He tried not to let that rattle his confidence.

"I think I'd need to know what normal looked like," EDDIE admitted to himself, *"Before I can recognize broken."*

He let out a long slow sigh. At least he hoped that's what it sounded like.

He clambered up into the cockpit of the little glider, and slowly guided it out through the doors. It didn't take long to navigate his way to the dusty track that ran straight as an arrow beside the pipeline. Some time ago, when there was rain, and the road had been wet, someone had driven heavy equipment down this road, leaving the surface heavily corrugated. EDDIE was glad that he could float over the corrugations. Had he been in something with wheels he'd have had a rough ride, juddering all the way.

He scanned ahead as far as he could, but he couldn't see the end of the pipeline. It kept going and going and going. Did his own smallness make a difference in the way he viewed the world, EDDIE wondered? Would things that were big to him seem normal to others? Crafty wouldn't have found the warehouse door much of a challenge, EDDIE was sure. He was cheered by that. He was seeing everything with a little robot's eye view, the world was not as big as it seemed.

Still, there was a lot of pipe and this was a mighty long road.

"What a pity this thing doesn't have auto-pilot," EDDIE said.

"Hold the control sphere until you are at the speed and direction you require," Vosna told him, "Then let it go. It will remain in place until you touch it again."

"Seriously?" EDDIE asked. One thing he was learning about Vosna is that she didn't offer information until she was asked. Then it struck him, maybe that she couldn't, maybe it wasn't her place.

"Remember though, the faster you go, the faster you drain the batteries."

"And the sooner I'm walking. Right. Thanks, Vosna."

"You're welcome, EDDIE."

He set the glider to follow the road at a speed he inferred would get him to where he was going, as fast as he needed to get there.

Chapter 16

H ere and there EDDIE could see what might have been buildings lost in the undergrowth of the advancing forest. These patches of difference were surrounded by a coldness that hinted at long disuse. A thick patch of forest had been cleared directly ahead of him; he couldn't tell by what. The narrow road was wandering its slow way up a hill, not the least bit interested in getting to the crest any time soon. The hill didn't seem to worry his little glider. It was happy to work across or clamber up whatever terrain it met. The trees and scrub that had been crowding the edges of the roadway shrank back, to eventually reveal a plateau.

EDDIE gently grasped the silver sphere and eased the little craft to a slow, smooth, and dustless stop. Though he remained scrunched up in the vehicle's cockpit, he was able to look far across to the east. A wide scar had been carved into the forest; a narrow gash that grew, fanning out into a broad, deep crater, choked with debris.

"Oh, my." EDDIE could see piles of twisted metal, ceramics, glass, and plastic, piled in a heap in the middle of a humungous crater. Excited for a moment, EDDIE suspected he had found the cause of the pipeline's loss of flow, but a quick scan showed no damage to the pipes at all; barely a ding here, maybe a dent there, but that was all.

"EDDIE, what do you see? I cannot access your visual cortex."

EDDIE wasn't sure he wanted anyone rummaging around inside his inner workings, even if it was Vosna, who felt like an old and trusted friend.

"I think it's a crash site." EDDIE clambered down from the glider and began to pick his was across the roughed-up terrain. "It looks like a plane crashed here?" He wasn't sure. He'd never seen a plane. He only had what was in his database to guide him, and Crafty hadn't managed to populate that fully before EDDIE had been whisked off with the Muk'Vuh.

"No, it was bigger than a plane." EDDIE revised his opinion, as he could see two huge engine cowlings lying ten or twelve meters apart.

"Was it a space craft?" EDDIE wondered.

EDDIE could sense Vosna's excitement even at this distance.

The terrain between EDDIE and the tangled mound of wreckage was rough, and he found it hard going. He considered going back for the glider, but he hesitated. He didn't want to take the little craft too far into this field of destruction. He picked as easy a path through the broken, shattered and burnt pieces as he could manage. There was something he wanted to confirm.

Some of the metal fragments showed off their stress lines. EDDIE poked at something with his foot. It felt warm. That might have been from the sun, rather than any residual heat from the crash. He could see evidence of a fire, but there had been a much greater heat source here, perhaps even the heat of re-entry. It had scorched deep into the metal, the ceramics, and tiles, that lay scattered about like some mad unfinished bathroom renovation.

Whatever the huge, ruined craft was it was fit for scrap.

EDDIE stopped suddenly. Ahead of him, off to one side, and not far from the tree line he could see three mounds of newly turned soil. Someone had taken the time and care to place a layer of carefully selected stones on top.

"They buried them, and then they followed the pipeline." It was obvious enough; they would have realised that the pipes supplied something to someone. It made sense that at the end of the pipes, there would be some sort of city. Somewhere they could find help.   Except the city at the end of this pipeline was slowly dying. They wouldn't have found the new home they were looking for.

They are explorers, or colonists, and they crashed, and they found themselves here, a long way from home.

EDDIE looked north. The pipeline kept going. There wasn't much more he could do here. At least now he knew where the Muk'Vuh had come from.

"EDDIE," Vosna's asked. "What have you found?"

"I think the Muk'Vuh ship crashed," EDDIE found his voice struggling to modulate, choked with another unfamiliar emotion. "For whatever reason. Three of them died. Now the rest are stranded."

"Like me, longing for a home they may never see again." It added to EDDIE's sense of urgency and obligation. So what if the Muk'Vuh had tried to eat Crafty's cat? That didn't matter now. Somewhere deep inside EDDIE was the feeling that it was up to him to help. In whatever way he could, regardless of how small he might be, he knew he had to give it his best try.

He turned and made his way back to where he had parked the glider, his steps more certain than before, his resolve hardening into determination.

Once again EDDIE set the little glider moving along the road which now dropped steeply away from the plateau.

"If there was some way we could communicate with them," EDDIE mused. *"We might be able to help them."* He rummaged around and replayed some of the recordings he had of the Muk'Vuh when it had first appeared in Crafty's shed. It wasn't the most pleasant language to listen to, EDDIE admitted.

Every time EDDIE fed the Muk'Vuh's speech into the voice emulator the device dug its heels in and refused to give even a pale representation of what the Muk'Vuh might be saying.

"Thruk'Vik! Yek vah."

"Your penguin has gas."

"Sh'd'ek'ee gaa'kak."

"My armpits are itchy."

"Well, that hardly works," EDDIE felt his frustration rising.

"It seems that the Muk'Vuh tongue is far removed from any known language groups, so it has nothing to work with in its translation."

"What's the good of it then?"

"Usually, the voice emulator is more than helpful," Vosna defended the technology with some indignation.

"Successful intra-galactic diplomacy is not going to sizzle along with 'your penguin has gas!' and I'm not the least convinced they will be interested in the condition of my armpits!"

"That is true. Misunderstanding is not the best way to start negotiations," Vosna agreed.

"Let's face it, Vosna, I'm not the Muk'Vuh's favourite little robot. I doubt he sees me as having his best interests at heart."

"Even if you do?"

"Even if I do."

Chapter 17

T he plateau had given way to a long and gloomy valley. EDDIE only had the pipeline and the shadows for company. It wasn't long before the terrain began to rise again, and the pipeline followed the contours until it rose up almost vertically and vanished into the side of a mountain. EDDIE brought the glider to a skidding halt. Dust sprayed up from the road in a wave that crashed over the glider, and for a second or two EDDIE lost all visuals. With a nudge of the controls, EDDIE gently edged the little craft forward out of the cloud. He gazed upwards, following the run of pipes. They turned at right angles before they vanished into the stone.

At the end of the road, at the base of the hill, beside the pipes, was a ladder, bolted to the rock. Way up at the top EDDIE could see a small platform and a doorway. From where he stood, they looked a very, very long way up. Had Crafty programmed him with a head for heights he wondered? He didn't like the idea of flying but being several hundred meters up a ladder that was bolted to the side of a mountain was different. Right?

With just a second or two to calm his fluttering valves, EDDIE began to climb. He struggled with the spacing of the rungs, for they had been made for longer legs than his. More than once he found himself dangling by an elbow hooked over a rusty rung before he was able to get a foot somewhere useful and could settle his equilibrium.

Too often he found himself chanting: "Don't look down, don't look down!" He looked down, of course, and the bottom of the ladder telescoped away into a hazy distance, spinning slightly as it went. "Oooh, don't do that, that's not good." Instead, he looked up, and the top of the ladder seemed incredibly distant.

"The people who built this must have been spiders or limpets!" How did they do this without fall protection? Ropes, and nets, and safety harnesses and parachutes? Someone like Vosna wasn't the right shape for ladders either. He wasn't sure how far into the air the amber football could rise before she met her service ceiling. It would be way too distracting to ask her right now. He needed to keep climbing. He needed to get to the top before he seized up. He could be stuck forever on this ladder in the middle of an alien wilderness like some fancy Christmas bauble.

EDDIE was glad that no one was watching him. He didn't think he looked at all dignified. That's if anyone actually cared about a robot's dignity! Did people care about robots at all? EDDIE didn't know any other robots. He knew they worked in menial jobs, and he hoped for their sakes they weren't given brains enough to think about what they were being made to do. He knew that boredom wouldn't be a problem for robots that hadn't been told what they were doing was boring. There were bound to be some machines that were smart though. He wondered about them too. All they did was sit around and annoy people spamming them with ads. How did they manage to keep their dignity intact? They probably felt very important because they knew all about algorithms, but then they used their knowledge for spam! Even though EDDIE didn't know much about algorithms, he knew they could be misused.

As EDDIE clambered higher up the ladder the cross winds became stronger. That made him even more anxious. Instead of just dangling, he started to swing, left and right, left and right. His metal body clanked hard against the rungs a few more times: the metal of the ladder rang with the sound his collisions, a sad bell tolling across the silent landscape. He felt a dent or two mar his casing, scraping off some of his lacquer. Further up, the wind was swirling, and he began to rotate as well, first clockwise, then anticlockwise, then he spun in not so delicate spirals that threatened to pull his arm loose from its socket.

"Oh help!" said EDDIE. He wasn't enjoying this part of his adventure. All he could do was hang on until the wind settled, which it did, eventually. He looked up at the last few rungs. *I can make it! I know I can.*

By this time, of course, he had worked out how to navigate the distance between the rungs. The last few proved almost anticlimactic, and he suddenly found himself lying flat on the platform at the top, not daring to look down. He let out what approximated a whoop of exhilaration. He'd done it, but there was no time to celebrate. He could almost feel the city drying out, the last of its lifeblood evaporating.

EDDIE got to his less than steady legs. He felt his servo motors compensate and his wobbling stopped. The door in front of him was tightly closed. When was the last time anyone had opened it? EDDIE wondered.

"Vosna, I need a little help here?"

"Already working on it, EDDIE," she told him. "The door is stuck, or it's locked. Or both."

The wind had picked up again, and EDDIE felt it pushing against his back, swirling around trying to shove him sideways. If it got any stronger it would lift him up and toss him off the platform like an empty drink can.

"No one has used this entrance for a very long time," Vosna informed him. "But they wouldn't need to, it's for emergency access only."

"This is an emergency, Vosna! I need to use it," EDDIE pleaded, "Before I get blown away!"

EDDIE tried pulling on the handle. Nothing moved. The dark shadow on his wrist, almost forgotten, suddenly came to life and the nanobots marched down his arm and into the keyhole. There was a loud scraping sound. Something inside the door vibrated and clanked and clicked and the door opened enough for a small puff of stale air to escape and tickle EDDIE legs and chest.

The nanobots emerged from the keyhole and returned to their place on EDDIE's wrist, a band of close-fitting shadow once again.

"Perhaps you could give it a hard tug," Vosna suggested.

It doesn't need to open all the way for me to slip through, EDDIE admitted. *I'm only little.* He wasn't sure how one small robot was going to make much difference to one big door, but he had to give it a go. It was strange, he reflected, how small this huge door had seemed from the base of the ladder.

EDDIE wedged himself against the door jamb and gave it his biggest teeth straining, eye-popping, cylinder jarring shove. He felt a mountain's weight worth of resistance, and he was beginning to think it was never going to move, but suddenly it gave way, and he toppled forward, across the threshold and into a lightless room that smelled like thousand-year-old socks.

There was grit on the floor that irritated his already offended casing. As quickly as he could, EDDIE scrambled to his feet.

"Lights on," he commanded, but the darkness remained.

"There should be a switch somewhere," Vosna said helpfully.

EDDIE began blindly patting his way around the wall before he remembered he could switch his micro-cameras into night vision mode. EDDIE quickly located the switches next to the door on the far wall and toggled them on. "That's got it." Once the lights were on, EDDIE could see that the room was empty except for a desk, a chair and old computer terminal, its screen dark slate grey.

"Something tells me this is not the main control centre."

"Of course not, silly!" Vosna chided him.

EDDIE felt a brief pulse of relief. He doubted that even the skills of Engineer, First Class could have cranked this old thing back to life. He ran a metallic finger along the top of the screen, feeling some empathy for redundant technology. At one time or another it would have been considered state of the art. But now it was little more than e-waste.

EDDIE took a final look around. He reminded himself he still didn't know what he was looking for. *"I'll know it when I see it, I'm sure,"* he said to himself, confident that whatever it was, wasn't in this room.

Chapter 18

E DDIE stepped out into an unlit passageway. Something had fallen from the ceiling and lay in big enough clumps on the floor, that EDDIE had to step around them. Relying on his infra-red night vision, EDDIE made it to the end of the hall. There was a door to his left. He pushed it open and stepped onto a metal landing at the top of a set of metal stairs. He peered over the railing, down into a heavy darkness. How far down the stair went he had no idea. He knew he didn't want to make his way down into the unknown. He scanned ahead as best he could, but there was too much metal, and his signal bounced around like a ping pong ball and everything came back to him as a fuzzy, blurry grey mess.

Heaped upon this was the silence, as deep as a tomb. Did he hear something stirring below him, on the utmost edge of his sensor's range? Was there a flurry of movement down there in the dark? Not a small flurry. But a big flurry. Maybe even a very big flurry. What caused that? Was it some mutant rat who had known nothing but darkness all its life? What was a defenceless little robot going to do against a huge, fat hungry rat determined to chow down?

"Come on EDDIE," he reminded himself. *"You haven't seen anything pretending to be wildlife, let alone rats."*

One of his integrated circuits stubbornly refused to let go of the image of a ravening rat in the shadows, but EDDIE refused to give in to his fear. "Bother that," he said firmly and took a tentative step, down one riser, with a loud, echoing clank. It reverberated into forever, bouncing off surface after surface until it eventually died to an offended silence somewhere far below, in the empty deep.

He stopped on the next half-landing. Below him, he could see the door to the next floor. Should he exit here or further down? He clanked down the last few steps and cracked the door open to peer into what once might have been a large office. It was completely empty, gutted and left to rot. Dotted across the floor were power outlets and data network points. Overhead were strip lights, dangling from the ceiling frame. He thought back to the warehouse and its shelf-less, floating inventory. This mix of old and new, of then and now existing side by side niggled his sense of order. He liked things that were logical. He had been designed to work with recognisable patterns and make connections after all. This juxtaposition of the old alongside the new wasn't logical, and he wondered if it had anything to do with the flow?

He continued down another floor and stepped out into a shock of vertigo. Although the room had a solid white composite floor. In front of him was a floor to ceiling window that angled outwards. It looked down onto clusters of unknown machinery far, far below. It was jarringly different from the previous space. Here was something new and unfamiliar. Here there were no light switches, no power outlets, or network points. At the limits of his night vision, EDDIE could see the pipes poking out of the side of the mountain. From this distance they looked like matchsticks, and they dropped almost vertically to the floor, plunging into the top of an enormous oblong casing sandwiched between banks of pumps or motors. Any sense of the familiar had fled. EDDIE had no idea what he was looking at, let alone what it did.

The scale of the place left EDDIE feeling extremely uncomfortable. He was too unsettled in his circuits to infer anything from what he observed.

In front of the window EDDIE noticed something that he hadn't seen when he first stepped into the room. Was it a thin glass panel, or plastic wrap stretched incredibly taught? From where he was standing it was almost lost in the reflection from the main window. He bunched up what he could find of his courage and stepped forward. Projected from somewhere that EDDIE couldn't see were images of gauges and dials landing on the transparent screen. One gauge, toward the middle of the panel showed several vertical bars. The bars were ticking away at the bottom of their range. EDDIE felt they should be registering much higher than they were.

"Those dials show the current condition of the flow," Vosna said, her voice loud in the silence. Startled, EDDIE jumped.

"You can see that the output is almost negligible. Before, when the city was fully alive, all of these would be close to the red line. That's when First Engineer's heart was most glad. When things were working the way they should. The way they were designed."

EDDIE wondered if this was a past that would come again, or if it would exist only as a memory in Vosna's mind?

"You must go down to the pump room floor," Vosna advised. To do what she didn't say. Perhaps she didn't know. "There should be a service lift nearby."

Indeed, there was. Together EDDIE and Vosna located it directly across the corridor and to the right. Its doors were slow to open, weary with lack of use. They closed with an unpleasant thunk, and the floor gave a shudder as the cage began to descend, very slowly. It took such a long time to get to the bottom, that EDDIE began to suspect that he wasn't moving at all.

Much to his relief, the lift door finally decided to open; but not smoothly. Everything had stopped working smoothly. Would there be a time when everything stopped functioning? Would Custodian cease to be whatever Custodian was? Would Archive shut down with all its ancient secret knowledge lost? It seemed to EDDIE that this terrible scenario could eventuate. Everything would be dead. What would happen to Vosna? Perhaps when the flow finally came to its last trickle, she would also fade to nothing. EDDIE was pained by that thought.

The pump room was almost silent. It was vast, and it should have been full of noise; so loud that EDDIE had to dampen his senses to prevent damage to his circuits. But there was no need for that. He could hear something ticking faintly, as if cooling and winding down, or marking time. Probably not that, after all, it seemed as if time itself had almost stopped.

EDDIE tried to calm the fluttering in his circuitry. He had to apply himself to solving the problem. He took a moment to settle his diodes. *What do I know about this situation?* he asked himself.

EDDIE was not an engineer, nor was he an expert on pumping stations, but it seems obvious to him, that if you tapped into an underground water supply, there would be enough pressure to start an inevitable and continual flow.

No, EDDIE thought, the flow had stopped for a reason; either the aquifer was exhausted, or something was blocking everything up. To EDDIE, this seemed obvious, it made sense.

Unsure of which way to go, he picked a direction at random, and proceeded along a bank of pipes and flanges. Here and there green fluid had dripped and splashed across the floor, crystallising as it fell. It gave off a calming green glow, making bright pools in his night vision. He picked his slow way forward. As he went the trail of green crystals gave way to jagged shards of brown, almost amber crystals, thrown carelessly across the floor; it was like powdered glass, or thick dust, and motes of it floated in the half light of his amplified vision. Another splash of amber had spurted out, crossing over and mixing with the first; different shades of ochre and brown flashed across his filters as he surveyed the array of debris on the surfaces around him.

He followed the trail of spatter on the floor and noted the spray that went up the sides of equipment and walls if there were walls nearby. It had fanned out from somewhere ahead of him. He felt a dread forming deep in his casing next to his valves. He came at last, to the clue that he hoped he would never see.

In front of him set in the floor, a maintenance hatch was flung open, and a ladder plunged down into the unknown depths underneath.

And beyond the hatch was something that startled him. It unnerved him. He tried not to look, but he saw it anyway.

Half in deeper shadow that his night vision couldn't quite penetrate, up against the far wall, beyond the open hatch, a football sized globule was floating in the air. It looked so much like Vosna, but it was not Vosna. Its bottom half had been ripped off at jagged angle, and there were glistening strands hanging from it, strands that were wet and ropey and grey.

Fanned out on the floor around it, were fragments of amber glass.

The amber globule was suspended in mid-air, but it wasn't moving. It was very, very still.

Chapter 19

E DDIE focused on what he needed to do and sidled over to the gaping maintenance hatch. The last thing he wanted was to make the acquaintance of another ladder. He stared down into a somewhere that was narrow and dark. At the edges of his vision, almost at the bottom of the hole he could see a pale-yellow light, strobing gently.

"Just another country stroll," he said, as if that would calm his nerves and convince his reluctant circuits to follow through with the plan that was forming within him.

Vosna was strangely silent. She hadn't spoken in ages. He considered reaching out to see if she was still there and watching through whatever cameras she had access to, but he decided not to say anything. It was better that she wasn't troubled by the visions that were slowly forming memories in his positronic mind. *"Can a robot un-see the things he doesn't want to remember?"* EDDIE mused. *"Can anyone?"* Is time something that helps memories to truly fade away to nothing, or are there some memories that stay, etched deep and forever? Maybe those memories need to be remembered, and brought to mind occasionally, to remind you of things that should never have been?

EDDIE pushed that consideration as far away as he could manage.

After a moment or two gathering up his courage, he stepped out and down onto the first rung of the ladder. To his relief the rungs were closer together than on the last ladder he had climbed. He tried not to think about the fact that someone or something had opened the hatch and had gone down into the underneath before him and may still be down there. He knew a saying that said fortune favoured the brave, he wasn't sure what happened to the foolhardy, and he didn't want to know just now.

It was difficult to keep the clunking of his metal feet to a minimum. If only he had thought to wrap his feet in cloth, he chided himself. There must have been old oil-soaked rags lying around somewhere in this vast space, but he wasn't about to go back up to look. If he alerted whoever was down there to his approach by his clanking descent, what choice did he have? Down he went, daring to hope that if they were still down there that they would not be hostile. Down into an ever-thickening darkness that, rung by rung clung heavier and tighter to his outer casing. He would have shivered if he was able.

Oh, Crafty, I wish you were here with me.

EDDIE would have whistled or sung a song. After all, isn't that what people did when they were scared? But he didn't sing, he kept clanking down the ladder, hoping that at the bottom, waiting for him to step off that last rung wasn't a large hungry rat. At long last his foot struck the final rung and, he stepped down into a shallow puddle of spreading phosphorescence, fanning green and bright around his toes. "No rats," he noted happily, with a deep sense of relief.

"Where to now?" He wondered. Not that there was much choice: It was either forge ahead or chicken out and go back up the ladder. "No one wants a robot chicken," EDDIE decided.

The passageway sloped gradually but inexorably downward, plunging ever deeper into the heart of the planet. There was water everywhere, pooling on the floor, around his feet, flowing down the walls and dripping from the ceiling. It was splashing on his head, forming droplets on his eyes, and making halos of whatever weak and yellow lights there were. If he spoke, he was sure he would have gurgled. Now, as wet as he was, he might be able to communicate with the Muk'Vuh with some success?

"Vosna?"

The only reply he received was static.

The maintenance tunnel dragged itself along, following natural contours in the rock, seldom running straight, as if it wasn't sure where it was going or what it was meant to do when it got there. Amazingly it opened out into a chamber that was well lit and bone dry. The surprise of it stopped EDDIE in his tracks. Along the wall, set about a meter apart were many valve handles. Every handle had been pulled hard left: except one.

Suspended above the dry floor, in the centre of the room was a large, shiny screen, with a blinking cursor that seemed to draw EDDIE forward.

"Vosna?"

"EDDIE! Oh, EDDIE, I thought I had lost you. Where are you? I can hear you, but I cannot see you."

"Honestly, I have no idea. I am somewhere underneath. I went down a ladder, and along a wet corridor. But how is it I can hear you?"

"Your voice emulator is linked into the system," she explained. "For some reason I wasn't picking you up until now." She sounded puzzled.

EDDIE approached the console. He could see lines of text tracing their way across the screen, but it was text he couldn't read. Underneath the screen was a keyboard of some sort, with back lit keys, that pulsed brightly then faded out. They followed some pattern; fading in and out from top left to bottom right, deepest red to the darkest blue, eight by eight and in the middle a small round key that had no colour at all. The central key was shining with a soft steady white light. On each key was printed a symbol, presumably it was an alphabet, but one that was totally unknown to EDDIE.

"Vosna, are there cameras in this room? Can you see this?"

"Yes, EDDIE, but they are old cameras. I can see the room, but not very clearly. From what I can see, the symbols are unfamiliar to me. The keyboard is not original tech. I can guarantee you that. I am surprised they got it to connect in the first place."

EDDIE nudged the keyboard with a finger, pushing it gently aside, revealing the console's inbuilt keyboard underneath. He glanced behind him, feeling an odd itch, as if he sensed the owner of the keyboard was about to step through the door. Nothing moved in the space beyond, and EDDIE returned his attention to the console.

On the screen EDDIE could see a line of indecipherable text, at the end of which was a flashing cursor: a vertical bar, flashing insistently, waiting for the operator's input. EDDIE's emulator gave him no translation, and EDDIE had no Rosetta Stone or translation key. He had to rely on Vosna to make sense of it for him. He tried his best to wait patiently.

"EDDIE, I think I've found it," Vosna chimed in. "It is some kind of subroutine, perhaps a really old one, it's trying to trigger a restriction in the flow. But that's not possible. There isn't a software control for flow management. The flow comes straight out of the aquifer, and there is no need to restrict it. We want to keep it flowing. Everything lives because it flows. That's just the way it is."

EDDIE took that information on board. "Perhaps there isn't software control. But there is manual control." EDDIE said, and he looked up to the valve handles.

"There is something here that doesn't make sense," Vosna said, sounding confused.

EDDIE agreed with her. It seemed that the flow from the aquifer could be closed off from this control point, and only from this control point, and only by using the valves on the wall. He tried to imagine what kind of emergency would demand that an operator shut the whole system down? Vosna was right, they needed to keep the whole thing flowing. After it came up out of the ground the first step was to pump it up and into the pipes and then let gravity take over; from there, without further intervention it would find its way into the city's reservoir.

"So, what can we conclude from all this?" EDDIE asked.

"Well, I suspect that someone has hacked into the system. The user is logged in as 'Technician.' And the system is waiting to be restarted in safe mode. *Or* confirmation of complete server shutdown!" Her voice was full of confusion. "EDDIE, there is no such person as 'Technician.' That user doesn't exist!"

Chapter 20

T here is no one I know of called 'Technician.'"
She paused to let that sink in.

"As far as I know, putting the system into safe mode, is for catastrophic emergencies only. And that has never happened before. Ever."

EDDIE looked down at the strange keyboard. He traced the cable from its side to where it disappeared under the console. He didn't have to lean too far over to see that someone had jimmied an access panel and had spliced the cable from the keyboard into the console's internal wiring. But there was more: another, much thicker cable ran from under the console, across the floor to the opposite wall. There it had been connected into a control box, the face of which had been pried off. EDDIE followed the conduit that ran from the control box, up the wall, and vanished into the ceiling.

"EDDIE, I can't find a way of logging Technician out of the system. I can't change user! They have come in using an unknown back door into the system software. I don't know how they've done it, and I can't undo it. I just don't have that knowledge!"

EDDIE could sense her distress. In an effort to sooth Vosna, he voiced the only logical suggestion that he had come up with so far. "What would happen if we gave it what it wanted? What if we let it reboot in safe mode?"

Vosna considered this for a moment or two. "It would take several minutes to get everything back up to speed. There would be flow again, straight into the turbine for hydroelectrics, the pumps would kick in and off we'd go. In theory."

"Would there be any disadvantages?" EDDIE asked, knowing there is usually a downside to these things.

"We would only get limited flow, until we were able to diagnose the issue correctly, and fully restart the system. Except ..."

"Yes?"

"I can't say until we do it, but I feel there may be a time limit, until safe mode automatically invokes a restart."

"That's not such a problem, is it?"

"Well, it shouldn't be, except that we don't really know what Technician was up to, and we won't know what damage has been done until we run a full diagnosis. That might take weeks! And if everything restarts normally, if it even does restart, we might be in an even bigger mess that we are now!"

EDDIE had a sinking feeling in his chest.

"And," Vosna went on. "It would have been First Engineer who would have overseen the process. He would decide what we needed to change after we had run the diagnostics. But I don't know where First Engineer is. He disappeared about the time of the noise. I haven't seen him since then!"

EDDIE wondered how he was going to conceal the truth from Vosna. He hoped she never saw what he had found upstairs. He didn't want to think about it. She was a friend, and he didn't want to see her hurt, but he had to wonder if any good would come from concealing such a hard truth? He had no idea, and he didn't want to find out.

"Let's enter a Y, or whatever the equivalent is, and see what happens," EDDIE hoped he sounded a lot more confident than he felt.

"Yes, I suspect you're right," Vosna said. "But it has never been done. Never. Yet, I agree, safe mode is better than a complete shutdown. Some system is better than none at all! It's got to be better than what is happening right now."

EDDIE gazed down at the flashing cursor. "Is it something I can do from here? Or do you have to do it from your end?"

"EDDIE, you have to do it from there. Use the original keyboard. Hopefully it hasn't been bypassed completely."

"You'll have to help me out here, Vosna. What do I type? I don't understand the lettering."

"There should be six rows of keys, each with eight keys."

"Yes."

"Third row down. Fourth key from the left. Press it."

EDDIE pressed it. He watched letters flow across the screen and then stop. The cursor was flashing at the end of the row once more, waiting for the next instruction.

"That's good," Vosna said. "Fifth row, the very last key."

EDDIE tapped it.

For a long time, there was no change at all on the screen. It was as if the system was waiting for some other action to take place.

Another row of text appeared on the screen.

"It says to open flow valves manually and confirm," Vosna read.

EDDIE once again looked over to the valve handles along the wall. Quickly, before he could lose his courage, he walked to the valve on the far left. The lever was stiff, as if it hadn't been used in a long time, and it took more effort than he was expecting, and he had to strain his servomotors almost to maximum before the handle slowly began to move. Seconds of hard pushing and it finally thunked to its fully open position. EDDIE moved to the next lever. And the next. And the next. One by one he thunked them into the open position. The servo motors in his arms and shoulders began to protest. He could feel them heating up with the effort of pushing each lever, but he was getting somewhere; he could sense it. He couldn't stop now. He hoped that his servomotors were up to the task, that they wouldn't burn out before he opened the last valve. Each time he opened a valve the walls would shudder as the flow returned to the pipes he could see as well as the ones he couldn't see.

Finally, the fifth lever clunked open. Why did Technician leave the last one, the sixth, untouched, EDDIE wondered? Quickly he went back to the console in the centre of the room. "Third row, fourth key," he reminded himself.

"Fifth row, last key," Vosna corrected him as his silicone tipped finger hovered above the keyboard.

He pressed the key.

A single word appeared on the next row down. The cursor flashed at the right-hand end before dropping down to the blank line underneath.

"Done," EDDIE said, although he wasn't convinced that he had made anything final.

"EDDIE, upstairs quickly," Vosna urged him. "You will have to manually restart the pumps. The turbine should start working on its own."

As quickly as he could EDDIE returned to the ladder. He stared up at the hole in the floor far above him. There was no way he was going to get there quickly. Why was he such a little robot? If he could somehow float up to the top, that would make life so much easier, but he had to do it the hard way, one rung at a time.

"Hurry EDDIE, hurry."

"I'm going as fast as I can, Vosna."

He edged past the floating amber teardrop, cold and still, the grey ropy strands hanging closer to the floor than they did when

EDDIE first saw it. All the lights had come on and were working up towards their full brightness level. It wouldn't be long before there were no shadows left at all, and the secrets of every corner would be revealed. Somewhere inside EDDIE, something tied itself into a big knot, or that's what it felt like.

Up here, the hum of machinery was loud enough for EDDIE to have to dampen his audio input.

"EDDIE, oh EDDIE," Vosna said, and for a moment or two he felt panicked about what she had seen. "It's working, it's working!"

EDDIE could hear the whine of the turbine, and if he didn't get the pumps working the pressure would build to the point of …

"Don't think, just do," he told himself.

He was glad of the time he'd had to survey this space from the control booth above when he'd first arrived. He knew where the pumps were, he had seen them from the control room above. Fortunately, they were all bunched together at the pipe head. Each had a switch panel, and on each panel, there was one red button and one green one. EDDIE pushed his thumb hard onto the rubberised green blister on the first pump. He heard the switch clunk into place above the sound of the turbine. New power was now running through circuits that had long been cold.

He felt the floor shake as the first pump spun into action, forcing fluid from the turbine up the side of the mountain, and out into the pipeline beyond.

He stepped across to the next pump and pressed on the green rubber covered button. Again, the floor shook as the pump started up. He paused at the last pump, for there were three, one for each pipe. He flexed his hands, waggled his metal fingers, as if to release the tension he imagined he felt. "OK," he said and pushed the final green button.

Nothing happened. There was no resulting whir or shudder, no vibration to confirm that the pump was working.

EDDIE suddenly felt his heart sink down to his diodes. What was he going to do? This had to work. Everything depended on it. Vosna's whole world was relying on him getting the pump working.

Chapter 21

E DDIE processed through his panic, his relays clacking in alarm.

He wasn't going to let it beat him. He counted to three and pressed the red button. He heard it click. *Wait. It might have a reset time out. He let the seconds tick by.* "18 … 19 … 20…" *OK, that'll do it.* He pushed hard on the green button.

He felt no response from the pump.

"Oh, come on!!!"

"EDDIE?" Vosna asked. "What's wrong?"

Not now, not now. I need to focus… focus… focus. One … two … three … hard on the red.

Click.

"Please, please, work, just work would you." He wasn't sure that an act of will would make things happen, but it couldn't hurt either.

He pressed down hard on the green. Did he hear it click? He asked himself. The combination of the turbine and the two working pumps were putting out enough noise that he might not have heard it. He couldn't be sure. Could he? It might have been his imagination.

Click.

It was loud and emphatic, and unmissable.

"That was it!"

Around the flanges that joined the pipeline to the pump array EDDIE could see small green crystals starting to form, getting fatter, bulging, and quivering, and dripping onto the floor, where each landed and bounced with a tiny metallic plink.

"Yes, yes!" Vosna shouted. EDDIE pictured her bobbing up and down in her control room far away. "EDDIE, we have gone from 3%, to 9%, it's working. It's working!"

EDDIE's gaze tracked along the pipes as they disappeared up through the rock wall. Moments ago, they had been dry. Now they were flowing again, their volume increasing more and more as the system came to whatever threshold safe mode allowed. He knew that it wouldn't be full bore, but he hoped it was sufficient to begin the city's revival.

EDDIE imagined it flowing like water down a dust choked creek bed after a heavy mountain rainstorm, that caused a tsunami like flow, picking up whatever it found in its way, tossing it end over end, and carrying it, captive, helpless to escape the torrent, until it was tossed aside far downstream.

"14%!"

EDDIE followed the flow with his mind. Down the pipes, down to the end, down to the reservoir, down to where the Muk'Vuh had made their camp. "Oh no!"

"EDDIE? What's wrong?"

"I need to get back. I need to get back *fast!*"

"There's plenty of time, surely."

"No! There's not." EDDIE said, his tone was sharper than he meant it to be. "I have to get back there, now!"

"Well ..."

"Vosna, has the flow started showing your end? Can you see it yet?"

"No, not yet. But I'm sure it won't be long." She sounded expectant, almost cheerful.

"It will though, and soon." EDDIE said. "Too soon."

EDDIE felt an almost overwhelming sense of helplessness. It would take him eons to wend his way back out, down the ladder to where he had parked the glider. Longer again to retrace his path along that pipeline, even at full speed. He tried to calm himself. He had to make Vosna understand the danger.

"Vosna," he tried to keep his voice calm. "What are our flippy-floppy friends doing?"

"They are at the water's edge EDDIE, some of them are swimming, some of them are just lazing about on the grass. I think they went out looking for food, they seem to have a taste for the water plants that grow on the far side under the pipes ..."

"Under the pipes?"

The implications finally hit her.

"EDDIE, directly under the control booth, not far from the elevator that brought you down, you should find a circle etched into the floor. You won't miss it. It will be obvious. I have forgotten where it is exactly. If it's not there, search for it. They try to put these things out of the way, so they don't cause interference, and that they aren't tampered with."

EDDIE started scouting around. There was nothing next to the elevator. His memory twanged. He had seen it, over near the maintenance hatch which had taken him to underneath.

Over where he found ...

"Vosna?"

"Yes EDDIE?"

"There's something I have to tell you."

"What is it?"

Bother, there is no way of saying this gently, he realised.

"I think I know what happened to First Engineer."

She was obviously waiting for him to finish what he had to say. "I found someone who looks like you. Over near the maintenance hatch. He was ..."

"You're going to tell me he is dead? That's it isn't it?"

"Yes." EDDIE breathed the word so quietly that he wasn't sure she'd heard it.

Vosna let out a howl of raw sadness that EDDIE felt would never end.

"I'm so sorry," EDDIE said, wishing he could help.

"How? How did it happen? How did he die?"

"I don't know." As he spoke, he made his way around the machinery, to where he had seen First Engineer, floating in silence. He felt he needed to say more. "I know where he is. I have seen him."

EDDIE was sure this is where he'd find the mysterious circle, whatever its function. The light level had risen enough for EDDIE to deactivate his night vision, although he had almost forgotten he had it switched on. What he saw was grim. First Engineer hadn't been alone. EDDIE knew that. Now that he saw what was in the shadows that he had missed previously.

He could see it now in the brighter lights.

Scattered among the amber shards was confetti punched from coloured cloth. There were big clumps of it next to a strange, unknown device. Beside that were six tubes, with metal caps top and bottom. They looked like fuses to EDDIE. All of them were empty, except for one which was full of shimmering green liquid. The empty tubes were lined up in a neat row next to the machine. EDDIE looked at the device. A clear panel at the front showed some of the liquid inside it, other than that it's use was not obvious.

"Did this belong to Technician?" EDDIE wondered. It was different from anything else he had seen. He transferred as much of the scene into memory as he thought necessary, knowing that he might have to review everything that happened later.

EDDIE continued his search until he found what he was looking for. It was over against the wall, well out of the way, where it wouldn't cause interference.

"Vosna, I think I've found it." EDDIE moved closer. "There's a circular marking on the floor. It is pale pink and slightly raised. Is that what you mean?"

Had he heard some sound, some small catch of voice. "Vosna?"

"Yes EDDIE," she said, her voice thick as if she had been crying. "That sounds like it. Is it glowing?"

EDDIE peered at it. There might have been a soft shimmer. "Hmmm ... Maybe?"

"Hopefully it has enough power."

"OK. What do you need me to do?"

"Step into the very centre of the circle."

"What? Why?"

"Trust me EDDIE."

"Righto." EDDIE stepped into the centre of the circle, as he had been instructed. Almost instantly he was enveloped in a pale haze. His sensors went into meltdown. Everything thrummed. Pins and needles rampaged through his casing. Sharp stabbing sensations ripped across his circuit boards. His vision swam, with his micro-dot camera lenses fighting hard to retain any hint of focus. EDDIE felt the floor open up beneath him.

Then it was over.

Chapter 22

"What ... was ... *that*...?" EDDIE could hardly form the words.

"Translocator," Vosna's matter-of-fact reply sounded close by his right shoulder.

EDDIE swivelled his head, and the football sized amber teardrop that was his friend Vosna swam into focus, bobbing up and down with excitement.

"I wasn't sure it would work."

"Work?" EDDIE still felt tingling in his hands and toes, and an unpleasant fuzziness everywhere else.

"Translocation, yes."

"How come you never mentioned this before?"

"It wasn't an option," Vosna explained. "With the power levels as low as they were the results could have been ... disastrous. Anything might have happened. You might have been turned into a cloud of vapor!"

EDDIE did not like the sound of that at all, but he did feel slightly miffed at having had to spend hours riding in a glider that wasn't designed for robots his shape if he'd been able to translocate instead. He suddenly felt mean because it wasn't Vosna's fault. She was doing everything in her power to help, he was convinced of that.

Yes, it had been fast, and he was thankful for that, but with the residual prickling in his innards he wasn't sure it would ever become his favourite mode of transport. He did his best to shake some sense of reality back into his valves. "The water will start flowing through those pipes very soon, and it won't be long before this reservoir is full to overflowing. When it gets to that the Muk'Vuh will be like frogs through a fire hose."

Vosna looked at him blankly. She had no idea what a frog was, let alone a fire hose. EDDIE did and it gave him the shudders. He wouldn't wish that fate on anyone, even a flippy-floppy, goopy Muk'Vuh. It wasn't in his heart to see that happen.

EDDIE wasn't so sure Vosna felt the same way. "Well, I suppose we could shoo them further up the bank to where it's safe," she suggested, "And then rescue any that get caught up in the overflow."

"Except neither of us are exactly equipped for water sports," EDDIE observed. "Unless you hadn't noticed."

"Well ... let me see. If you can't swim, you could fly!"

"Fly?"

"Oh yes, of course. Engineers use ion propulsion packs all the time."

The little glider was bad enough; EDDIE was not designed to be a friendly fit for equipment used by Engineers, Second Class or otherwise. "I'm not sure how that's going to work. I'm built more like a Milo tin than a jellybean!"

Vosna drew back at EDDIE's tone.

"I'm sorry Vosna, I didn't mean that."

He felt that she was eyeing him up and down; although he still wasn't sure where her eyes were. And she didn't seem the least bit upset at being likened to a jellybean. "We would have to make some modifications; I'll grant you that. You *are* an unusual shape, after all." She sounded more positive than EDDIE felt. They had come so far; he didn't want to give up now. He wasn't going to give up now. "*No*," he said to himself. "*We must make this work. Somehow.*"

"I am not going to give up now!" He would not let the Muk'Vuh suffer such a horrible fate.

"I trust you're the Engineer for the job, Vosna," EDDIE told her. "Whatever we do, we must do it quickly. Though, I fear we may not have as much time as we'd like." He could see the pipes in the distance, more clearly than he had before. More of the lighting had come back on and the cavern wasn't as dark as it had been. Already the flow was more than a trickle, it had swollen into a steady stream.

"Come," she urged EDDIE, "Come." And she was out the open door in an amber flash.

EDDIE put on as much speed as his little legs would allow. Had he been human his lungs would have been working like bellows and his legs burning like lava with lactic acid.

EDDIE paid little attention to where they went. He trusted Vosna, and he knew she knew the way, so he followed her. It was hard keeping up, and he was relieved when finally, she came to a halt. She was standing in a doorway to one of the pods on the shore opposite the Muk'Vuh camp; EDDIE could see them milling around on the bank. They were pointing to the steady flow that was coming from the pipes, and there was animated discussion going on. The Muk'Vuh with the beetroot-coloured crest seemed to be in conference with the other leaders if that's what they were. EDDIE didn't have time to worry about the leadership structures of Muk'Vuh society at the moment. Right now it was their safety he was interested in, not their pecking order. Whatever they were discussing, the leaders weren't happy, but Beetroot seemed to be in charge.

As EDDIE watched, the flow started to form defined cascades. It wouldn't be too long before there would be a noticeable increase in the water level of the reservoir, and then the real panic would start to set in. When water started to tumble over the spillway of the dam, chaos would ensue. EDDIE hoped there was still time enough before the flow got to that intensity, when it would set up a rip tide and start dragging unsuspecting Muk'Vuh into the water and across the dam wall and down to a roiling, churning, choking death below.

EDDIE watched Vosna as she darted from place to place, gathering pieces of equipment, and dumping them into a pile at

EDDIE's feet. He could see some sort of harness with a tank attached. There were coils of wire and what looked like rolls of duck tape! *That was getting a bit too close to the aquatic! At least ducks can swim*, EDDIE thought despondently, *robots can't.*

"One last thing," she said confidently, "and I should have everything I need."

Vosna spent an uncomfortably long time sifting through bibs and bobs in a rack in the far corner. She did not find what she was looking for. Making a "hmpf" sound, she said, "Stay here," and sped back the way they had come. Down into the maze of passageway's she knew well. EDDIE found himself wondering how many engineers might once have used these corridors?

Where had they come from? EDDIE wondered. Were they robots like him? She didn't seem like a robot. Had she had been put together by a program that ticked away on a server hidden somewhere far underground? Could more engineers be created and commissioned? Was there a blueprint for engineers to be discovered deep in Archive, with Custodian's help? Other than Vosna and the engineer he had seen back in the pump room, there were no others? As far as EDDIE knew, Vosna was the only Engineer left. Once he returned home, she would be alone, and that wasn't a happy thought.

Vosna zipped back into the room and deposited another bundle of equipment onto the pile. EDDIE peered down at one of the items in the pile. "Is that a joystick?"

"Old technology," she said with a jiggle, which EDDIE assumed was her equivalent to a nod. "I had difficulty finding that. I'm hoping it works as a controller. These harnesses work on the skin currents of the engineers wearing them. Sort of like the glove control on the glider. But different. I wouldn't know where to start rigging you for that. Even if I could, I don't think we'd have time."

Finally, she has realised the urgency of the situation.

She bobbed back and looked him over for the thousandth time, measuring him up. "Yes, yes, I'm positive, we've got this."

With that she set to work.

Chapter 23

E DDIE tried to keep his arms and legs from getting tangled in the dozen loose straps of the harness. Vosna was doing her best to wrangle it into place, so she could fasten it to the polished surface of his chest.

"Hold still," Vosna said. "You're wriggling."

"I'm trying not to!"

"Fidgeting," she said, "That's what you're doing!"

EDDIE was starting to feel like a flowerpot in a macramé hanger.

Vosna had spent a lot of time moulding an armrest for the joystick. From somewhere she had found a length of white composite, but it wasn't soft enough to bend to the shape she wanted, and when she had tried to force it, it sprang back and whacked EDDIE in the mouth.

"Ow!"

"Sorry."

"I have to heat it to soften it and get it in the right shape. It won't work like this."

Any thought of the pipes made EDDIE nervous, and he was thinking of them right now. They were nowhere near full flow, he knew that. They would never get to that point while the system was in safe mode, but their current output was going to make things challenging before too much more time passed.

Vosna was setting up some sort of coil on the workbench. With a bit of effort, extruding several of her tendril like arms in the process, she managed to form the composite into the shape she desired. Or close enough to it.

EDDIE observed all this and tried not to give way to his doubts.

"That'll have to do," Vosna declared, bobbing back. The super-heated coil that she had been using to soften and shape the composite, faded to a deep charcoal grey colour as it cooled. EDDIE had no idea how Vosna didn't get burnt during the process.

"First Engineer said, *'a time for a need and a need for a time.'*" Suddenly she stopped. "How do I know that?" It was not a question she could answer. "Our job as engineers is to make things work. That's what First Engineer would have said, if he was here," she went on, a light catch of sadness in her voice.

She carried on in silence for a few moments, flitting around EDDIE in an amber blur. Once or twice, she made noises of concentration or frustration, or both. She patted a last little piece of duck tape in place and bobbed back, to survey her handiwork. "And, at the end of the task, an engineer can take satisfaction in having executed an almost perfect solution for the situation."

There wasn't a huge lot of articulation in EDDIE's range of movement to begin with. There was a lot less now with all the straps and tape. He could lift his arm above the composite arm rest and with a bit of a jiggle he managed to find a position for his hand that wasn't too twisted up. With a bit more experimentation he was able to grip the joystick and hopefully operate it.

"Hardly elegant," Vosna admitted, watching his contortions. "But I think it will do the job."

EDDIE wasn't sure about any of it, but he kept quiet. He suspected the gaps he felt here and there in the harness were part of the compromise Vosna had to make because of his shape. Every time he moved, one of the straps that was hanging loose slapped against his casing. It wasn't comfortable, but it didn't need to be. It needed to do the job.

A cry of alarm echoed across the water.

EDDIE and Vosna darted out of the maintenance pod and saw that three, now four of the Muk'Vuh were floundering in the water. The placid surface hid the current that was starting to stir and to pull towards the spillway. On the bank the Muk'Vuh were darting up and down, yelping in alarm. They were wading into the shallows before backing out again, as they sensed danger and felt the tug of the current.

EDDIE tried putting on a brave face. Crunch time, he thought, and immediately regretted reminding himself of the possible consequences of this venture. *"I am not going to end up in a tangled heap of scrap,"* he assured himself.

"Are robots really meant to fly?" EDDIE gulped. It took him a bit of effort to jiggle around so that he was facing the dam rather than the doorway of the shed. Slamming into the side of the shed on his maiden flight wasn't part of the plan.

"Perhaps it would be wise to move forward a bit?" Vosna suggested.

"I'm not sure I can," EDDIE replied.

He tried hopping, but almost fell over backwards. Vosna's acted quickly. She got behind him and gave him a gentle shove that saved him from landing flat on his back like a tortoise, with arms and legs waving around in useless arcs in the air.

"Here and here," Vosna pointed to the master control switches. "The joystick should make things easier for you. At least you don't have to wrangle two handles. Not like the old days."

"Right," EDDIE agreed, thankfully, not sure how he was going to work with one handle, let alone two.

"Pay attention would you?" Vosna said sternly. "Roll, like this? Left, and right. Yes? Pitch, like this? Forward, back. Got it? Good. Yaw, like this? Twist left and right. Super. You're a natural. You will have this down in no time."

EDDIE had no idea at all what roll and pitch were, let alone yaw, but there wasn't time to figure them out. Time for raw instinct to kick in. *"Don't think, just do, trust your programming."*

EDDIE examined the makeshift controls methodically. "Throttle?" he asked feeling bemused and uncertain.

"Yes, this little lever here," Vosna said, pointing with a tendril.

The harness tightened around him as EDDIE nudged the throttle lever forward. The contraption hesitated, communicating its reluctance, before he felt his feet lift a centimetre or two off the ground. *I must weigh a lot more than an engineer.* He struggled with the awkward angle of his hand, but with a bit more effort, he was able to get sufficient grip to manage pitch and roll. Yawing on the other hand proved a near impossible challenge. How would he ever get all these things working smoothly together?

Without warning the propulsion units kicked like a mule, and he shot upward, spinning as he went.

"You've gotta be kidding!"

His dangling legs began to flail as he rotated.

"EDDIE!" Vosna cried.

"Oh, grief," EDDIE said. "I've turned into an eggbeater!"

"No! Don't push forward," Vosna called to him. "Oh! My goodness. No! Less twist! Less ... ah, right, yes, now a bit less throttle. No! Pull it *back*. No. The other back! Silly robot."

He knew Vosna was trying to be helpful but having her barking instructions was only making things worse. Was yaw up or down, or left, or right? He thought he'd worked out roll, but too much, and he would tumble end over end like some flopsy doll at a fair ground, tossed away by a careless child.

"I'm confused!" EDDIE admitted, and he was starting to feel sick. He could feel his stabilizers turning an unpleasant shade of pea green.

After wrestling with it for a minute or two, he found himself hovering almost upright some two meters from the ground, just at the edge of the lake. Thankfully, Vosna had finally given up on her commentary. Instead, she had decided to let EDDIE work through the control system on his own.

EDDIE's gyroscope had been doing its best to help him to keep balance, but it was a struggle. Every now and again he lost any sense of up, or down. He had a reasonable idea of left and right. At least for now. Until everything inverted itself. He still didn't feel the least bit confident, but now wasn't the time to stop and think it through; now was the time for courage and action.

"Yeah, right."

The panic on the far shore had escalated. He could hear loud yelps and yips and cries, and gurgles and harsh, heavy grunts of fear. EDDIE had no real plan. From where he was hovering, he could see a young Muk'Vuh splashing furiously, fighting against the rip that was pulling it toward the dam wall.

Beetroot had seen the youngling's struggle. But Beetroot was too far away to get to the little one in time. "Gik nach uk nik gak!" *Whoever is close, help if you can!* EDDIE didn't understand Muk'Vuh but that much was clear.

"OK, let's go," EDDIE gritted his proverbial teeth and pushed the throttle forward, "Oh help!" He cried. "Robots are not meant to fly!"

Chapter 24

E DDIE felt a moment of pure terror as his hand spasmed on the joystick, and he started to rotate. For a second or two he was moving forwards and sideways at the same time. He did his best to right himself, but he lost altitude, and his toes were almost dipping in the water. He managed to wobble upward and somehow stabilized his forward flight.

"Is this really the best way of doing this?" he wondered. He looked down to the surface where there were now two Muk'Vuh struggling in the water; the youngling he had seen before and an older one who had gone in to rescue it. Whatever strategy they adopted; the end result must be the same for EDDIE: Getting the Muk'Vuh to safety before they reached the wall of the dam. After all, it was because of EDDIE they were in danger in the first place. He felt responsible. It was his fault. He had started the pumps. He no longer cared that Beetroot had tried to eat Mrs McKenzie. Without EDDIE's help right now, all of the Muk'Vuh faced certain death.

For a moment he wondered why these amphibians were such hopeless swimmers, but he knew that frogs don't fare too well in washing machines either, and other than their froggyness, he didn't know if the Muk'Vuh were amphibians.

"Yikes! Concentrate," EDDIE told himself as he lurched mid-air and somersaulted, and he found himself head down, tail up and wobbling around anti-clockwise.

"NO!" cried Vosna, "Fly straight, EDDIE, fly straight."

"What do you think I'm trying to do?" EDDIE said through gritted speakers. He felt the top of his head skim the water. The last thing he wanted to do was lose altitude and have to learn how to breathe underwater.

"Which way is up?" he wondered. "Does up even exist?"

Any idea of safety had long since evaporated from EDDIE's mind. He had to act fast. He wrenched the joystick in the direction opposite to the way he felt it should go. His gyroscope gave another nauseating heave and EDDIE was flying upright once again.

"Robots are definitely *not* meant to fly," he said miserably, wondering, not for the first time, how he had got himself into this.

The little Muk'Vuh closest to the dam wall was barely keeping its head above water. EDDIE guessed it was used to placid ponds not violent rapids.

EDDIE circled the youngling twice. The thrusters on EDDIE's harness chopped up the water. He dropped in altitude as low as he dared and was wondering how he was going to rescue the creature, when he felt small, slippery, wet, flippery fingers wrap around his leg. They fastened tight as a vice.

Instinctively he gave his leg a big shake, but the little one was too frightened to do anything other than hang on. Its grip was tighter than a limpet.

For a moment they dipped closer to the water, with the extra weight of the little Muk'Vuh dragging them down. The little one went under, and EDDIE saw its terrified eyes vanish under the waves. EDDIE battled the complexities of the joystick, and the little Muk'Vuh's trembling, dripping phosphorescent green body rose up and out of the water as EDDIE lurched unsteadily upwards and toward shore.

Eager froggy hands reached up and took the youngling into relieved froggy arms.

EDDIE did not pause.

There were even more heads bobbing in the water now, caught in the rising tide and the current, that was getting stronger. They were being dragged closer and closer to the dam wall and to the nearly vertical drop beyond it, to the churning water below.

EDDIE came in range of the next Muk'Vuh and lowered his right leg for the creature to grab. It did not hesitate. It latched on hard as a barnacle.

"I can take two," EDDIE assured himself. "I *must* take two."

He swooped in close and dangled his left leg for the Muk'Vuh to grab. This Muk'Vuh was bigger, and heavier, and EDDIE felt the extra strain on his already over-stressed chassis. With faith in Crafty's engineering and believing that nothing was going to give way or be ripped off, EDDIE lifted as smoothly as the extra weight would allow, and lumbered towards the shore, releasing the Muk'Vuh to safety.

"EDDIE, EDDIE," Vosna called, her voice loud in his emulator.

"Erm, I'm a bit busy at the moment, Vosna," he said, trying not to sound snappy. "Is it urgent?"

"Yes! Check the gauge, check the gauge!"

EDDIE looked around, wondering what she was talking about, and out of the very edge of his vision he saw a small strip of colour on the composite arm, half hidden by his wrist. It was working its way from orange to red.

"You must stay within safe limits," Vosna advised, "If the harness overheats, or runs low on charge..."

"Don't tell me," EDDIE groaned. "I don't want to know. Really, I don't!"

As he quickly surveyed the lake, he could see the heads of three more Muk'Vuh, bobbing in the water, moving closer and closer to disaster.

"Let's do this!"

Trying to ignore the coloured bars that kept grabbing at his attention from under his wrist, EDDIE again manoeuvred towards the surface and felt a single set of icy webbed fingers wrap about his leg. *Wow! This Muk'Vuh is heavy.* It was more than he had ever lifted, and way more than he wanted to lift, be he couldn't give up. He had to keep going. He worked the harness to its limit, feeling rather than hearing its whine of complaint as it strained every fibre and fuel cell. He barely managed to lift the Muk'Vuh into the air and realised there was no way he was going to be able to manage two on this trip. He would have to come back.

I need more time! I need more time!

EDDIE got to the shore as fast as the thrusters allowed, and as the Muk'Vuh let go, EDDIE felt something give way with a loud, wrenching, and utterly sickening *pop*.

"Ouch," he said, "Ouch," yet he didn't stop. He couldn't stop. No matter what had just broken loose, he had to keep moving.

The last two Muk'Vuh had been dragged to the dam wall by the current and were unhappily bumping their way along the inside of the wall toward the gaping void of the first of the spillways.

"Oh crikey!" EDDIE said.

He threw aside all caution and swooped low and fast and came to a hover as close as he dared to where the water had started to seethe and swirl close to the void. EDDIE clonked the nearest Muk'Vuh in the head with his foot to get its attention, as it was totally focused on trying not to drown. They didn't give EDDIE any choice. Both reached up as far as they could and gripped his legs, desperately tight, clinging hard, one on each leg.

EDDIE grimaced and opened the throttle to its shuddering limit.

Under his wrist the gauge had started to flash red, matching the alarm EDDIE felt within his valves.

"Move," EDDIE screamed at himself and the thrusters. "Come on, come one, move!"

EDDIE felt the engines cough, and he and the Muk'Vuh began a slow, inexorable plunge into the water!

Chapter 25

For the longest moment there was nothing but dead weight. The tanks were almost empty of propellent, he knew that much. But a thimbleful of fuel would do the job. He had to trust there was enough left to finish what he had started.

As if in defiance of EDDIE's hope, the little gauge stopped flashing. Now it was a solid, angry red.

"Come on. Come on. Just a bit more," EDDIE growled, willing the engines to give a smidge more lift; a little extra joule of thrust.

Slowly they began to rise, one centimetre at a time, then two; five; a whole meter. Then, like a cork out of a cannon they were airborne. EDDIE dared to glance ahead, and he felt his heart sink. The shore seemed so very far away.

There was another grinding, crunching pop, this time from EDDIE's other leg. *"Hold on. Hold on! You can fall off later when everyone is safe."*

The shore dragged closer, a millimetre at a time. Just as EDDIE dropped the last two Muk'Vuh into the waiting arms of their family, the thrust from the harness dwindled to little more than a puff of breeze. As if it knew it could, now that the last Muk'Vuh was safe, it faded to a final soft gasp. EDDIE dropped like an unwanted pebble onto the muddy shore.

EDDIE felt a swooping lift of joy rise up from somewhere deep in his chest. Totally unbidden, his soundbar emitted a whoop of happiness, and he relaxed in a huge puddle of relief, even as the Muk'Vuh began gathering around him. He could hear their voices, rising in a clamouring crescendo. He suspected that they were cheering. At least, he hoped it was that and not some war chant.

Suddenly they fell silent as the Muk'Vuh with the beetroot-coloured crest with the vibrant orange tips stepped into the circle they had formed around EDDIE.

"Yek'Nok yich nek goch kek vosh." With that the Muk'Vuh leader emphatically held out a webbed hand.

It was an effort, but EDDIE reached up and took the hand, and he was lifted up onto his wobbly legs. His gyroscope recognised that he was once again vertical and quickly made adjustments and the lurching wobble EDDIE felt settled to a bearable sense of dizzy.

"Robots are just not meant to fly," EDDIE said.

"Uk nech o noch yek." Beetroot said and made a sound that could have been a laugh.

The voice emulator gave a hesitant and belated burble. "Insufficient sample," it said sullenly. "Linguistic group unknown."

"Oh, right-o," EDDIE said.

"EDDIE, EDDIE," cried Vosna. "The flow, it's returning. The channels in the city, they are no longer dry, everything is starting to revive!!!"

In the far distance EDDIE felt more than heard a sound, like crystal chimes: each tone lifting higher than the last, to sing a song that was filled with celebration. It was ringing down long colonnades and through dry gardens and washing across piles of dry rubble. It was the wonderful sound of life returning.

"We did it, EDDIE, we did it!" Vosna's joy was almost tangible.

EDDIE's legs wouldn't let him stand without support, and he didn't want to rely on the Muk'Vuh for too long. "What do we do now?" he asked Vosna. He had hoped she was clued in on the damage he had taken. If she was, her answer gave no indication of her awareness.

"Now we make our way up to the surface."

There was a hint of wonder in her words. The surface. It was somewhere she had never been. She had been stuck for however long, in and around her control room, in the depths, doing the only thing she knew; faithfully doing her job as Engineer, Second Class.

Safe Mode was working well enough, and it would do for the time being. EDDIE couldn't guess how long that might be. Vosna was deliriously happy with the way things were, but EDDIE wasn't. He knew that safe mode could never be a permanent solution. It occurred to EDDIE that Vosna's understanding might be limited because of the limited time that she had been aware. Despite his comprehensive knowledge banks, EDDIE didn't really know anything from before Crafty had flicked his power switch, and he had come online. If Vosna was some sort of robot as EDDIE suspected, then she wouldn't have the faintest idea of what had happened to bring Engineer, First Class to the pump room. He wondered whether there was only meant to be one Engineer at a time? There were so many corridors and so many things to maintain he doubted that was true. With the death of the First Engineer, did the system activate a replacement? Had Vosna started her life the moment First Engineer ended theirs? Vosna seemed to remember First Engineer, up to a point. EDDIE wasn't sure how much of that was memory and how much was her programming. He was certain there was a mystery that needed to be solved before everything here could return to normal.

The waterline was continuing to rise, and the Muk'Vuh were moving up to where it was safe and dry. For the time being that's where they were happy to stay.

Vosna bobbed into view. She seemed to be brighter and slightly larger than he remembered. A gasp rippled through the Muk'Vuh gathering, and they all stepped back.

"It's OK," EDDIE tried to reassure them, "She's with me."

There was a round of yips and yelps which Beetroot calmed with a gesture of his flippy floppy hand; fortunately, it wasn't the one he was using to hold up EDDIE. With Beetroot's reassuring gestures, the Muk'Vuh let out the breaths they were all holding. They did not fully relax but settled into a calm watchfulness.

"Come," said Vosna, "Come."

For a moment Beetroot relaxed his grip, and EDDIE detached himself and did his best to step forward, but his legs crumpled underneath him. EDDIE toppled over and fell flat on his back. "Oh, bother," he said with feeling, as he gazed up at the arch of the cavern ceiling far above. He did his best to sit up but couldn't quite manage it. His legs were all tangled up, and refused to move at all, despite the flurry of commands EDDIE sent to them. After several long, agonising seconds, EDDIE gave up, realising that he was broken.

"EDDIE," Vosna bobbed forward, her skin rippling in bright colours of concern. "What's wrong?"

"My legs are broken," he said, telling Vosna what he knew to be the absolute, literal truth, which should have been obvious. In fact, they had been pulled completely out of their sockets by the weight of one too many Muk'Vuh. Now they were attached by little more than a few thin wires.

"Never mind," EDDIE said, trying to sound positive. "Nothing Crafty can't fix."

I need to find my way home!

The water level had started to lap at their toes. He knew they needed to move, now, while they still could, and before he short-circuited. If robots weren't meant to fly, they certainly weren't meant to swim.

Vosna was beckoning them forward, toward the huts.

For a moment no one moved. EDDIE looked at Vosna, then at Beetroot. The Muk'Vuh chief scooped EDDIE up under one flippy-floppy arm and moved towards Vosna. One by one the other Muk'Vuh followed, some glancing back at the black water, that was rising steadily, inexorably, accompanied by the sound of the water falling from the pipes, far away, echoing through the cavern.

Chapter 26

I t wasn't the most comfortable or dignified way to return to the surface and the city.

EDDIE hadn't been expecting a triumphant return, riding in on a chariot, with his ego all swollen with victory, like the old days of the Roman Empire. Instead, here he was, wending his way along on the transport platform, with his chest and back glistening with Muk'Vuh goop. It was not his most proud and defining moment. In fact, it was something he was never going to talk about. Ever. To anyone.

"Remember you are only a robot." The irony of this was not lost on EDDIE.

It took five trips of the elevator to get EDDIE, Vosna and all of the Muk'Vuh, safely to the surface. EDDIE had visions of the water starting to lap at the door of the maintenance sheds, down there in the darkness of the cavern. He hoped the shed doors were waterproof and wouldn't let any water into the maintenance corridors to cause flooding. He imagined that the water was now roaring over the spillway, down into the hydroelectric turbines, and further on, to the machinery that separated the water from the phosphorescent energy. From there, he knew, it was siphoned off, dark as green emerald to nourish Custodian, and Archive, flowing as the lifeblood of the city once again.

EDDIE wondered briefly if that lifeblood was what Technician had wanted?

The elevator door swished shut behind the final group, and they all stood blinking in the bright sunlight.

Vosna rippled as the pleasant warmth of the sun fell on her skin. "Oh," she said, softly. "That feels wonderful!"

Beetroot lifted his nose to the air and sniffed. "Huk vish nek, shu jeb noh!" he exclaimed.

He set EDDIE down, more gently and respectfully than EDDIE was expecting. Then Beetroot moved away, several flippy-floppy hops, toward the stippled shadow of the trees. Without a word, the others obediently followed, and one by one they vanished into the forest.

"Where are they going, do you reckon?" EDDIE wondered.

"If the water is flowing like it used to," Vosna said. "It's fair to say they're heading for the lakes beyond the gardens. It's not exactly home for them, but they will be safe enough there and ... happy. Yes, I hope they will be that too."

Vosna looked down at EDDIE. "You are a bit of a mess," she observed, bluntly.

"You think?" EDDIE wished he could smile. When he got back home, he would ask Crafty if that was something he could install. EDDIE felt that a smile might be useful to have.

Vosna examined EDDIE's legs for a minute or two. She bobbed back and made an "hmmm," sound. "I don't know," she confessed. "You are very strange technology."

"You'd have to talk to Crafty about that," EDDIE said.

"Perhaps one day I can have many interesting conversations with him," Vosna said.

"Right now, I'd be happy just to stand up, let alone walk."

"A time for a need, and a need for a time," Vosna declared. "I don't want to tinker with technology I don't understand. Even if you are the most marvelous and puzzling design."

EDDIE felt a flush of heat in his valves on hearing Vosna's flattery.

"There's still a way to go," said EDDIE. He was trying to be philosophical. At least the vital bits of him were working. *If your innards are still ticking along as they should, you're doing OK. If you need sticking plaster, bed rest and traction, so what?*

"Be of good cheer, EDDIE robot," Vosna said. "All is not lost. I have a amazingly good idea."

"*Well, that's hopeful,*" EDDIE thought.

"Wait right here," Vosna told him and cheerfully bobbed off along the path, sunlight glinting off her skin, or shell, or whatever it was she had.

"Okey dokes," EDDIE said. "Actually, I wasn't planning on going anywhere, at least not in a hurry."

Vosna did not seem to hear him. She was busy humming, harmony, and counterpoint. It floated through on the voice emulator, rising above and melting into the sound of the water flowing in the middle distance. The last note hung in the air for a long time before EDDIE was left alone in the hush of the afternoon. There was only so much lying on your back and looking up at the sky a little robot could take. Again, he did his best to sit up. It hadn't worked before, but he thought he'd give it another go. Toothpicks and teabags and optimism.

He considered a verse or two of "What shall we do with the broken robot," but that didn't seem appropriate somehow. He knew his voice would sound harsh and thin against the song of the phosphorescent energy that was flowing again through the city's conduits.

Up until now, EDDIE hadn't had the time to stop and reflect on anything that had happened since he found himself here. He had been busy with the doing. "I haven't done a very good job at being an *inference* engine," he confessed to himself. He had learned to trust his best guess, that was true, and so far, it had worked out, mostly, but that didn't mean he shouldn't plan to improve. He realised that he needed to infer more and act less quickly.

But I'm not the same robot I was when I left home. Was it yesterday? Or the day before? Or last week? It seemed as if he had been away for a long time, and he had come a long way, but he wasn't there yet, wherever there might be, and he wondered what might be waiting for him when he arrived wherever there was. So *long as there aren't any rats to snuffle around and sample me as their next meal, I'll be OK.*

"Do these kinds of adventures even have an end?" He wondered out loud. "Or does one adventure melt into another without a holiday in between?"

He heard Vosna long before he saw her. She bobbed back into view, carrying something EDDIE couldn't make out, engulfed as it was in a net of amber that hung suspended beneath her.

"Here I am," she said, "Back again," and she drifted out of sight behind him. He felt her jiggling the harness that was still duck taped to him. There was a solid metallic click, and he heard something hit the ground. "Hold still, would you, another moment and I should have it."

EDDIE saw the power gauge next to the joystick leap from reproachful red into a smooth and soothing green.

"If you aren't able to walk," Vosna told him happily, "The very least you can do is fly!"

"Oh joy," EDDIE sighed.

"This time, EDDIE," she told him, "I want you to do it *slowly*! You understand slowly, right?"

With a speculative touch, EDDIE tested the thrusters. There was a gentle response, and he lifted a few bare centimetres into the air. He feathered the joystick and slowly, almost regally turned full circle where he floated.

"Ahh, that's much better," Vosna told him. "You look like you are getting the hang of it!"

EDDIE quickly found the sweet spot, where there was a connection between his systems and the harness. How much of his new-found control was due to his lack of excitement, or stress? He wondered, or did it have more to do with the city coming to life once again? Its systems were coming back online, they were only a third of what they should be, yes, but life enough. The more energy intensive routines would stay offline, he knew, safe mode would see to that, at least for a time.

EDDIE gave the throttle the smallest nudge, and he drifted forward half a meter. He felt a feather of satisfaction tickle his diodes.

"I could get used to this," he admitted. As long it remained sedate, of course. "*I'll call it hovering*," he told himself, "*Not flying.*"

"Come," Vosna said. "It will do for now."

"Thank you Vosna, yes it will. Very much. It certainly beats walking on broken legs!"

"We should go, EDDIE," Vosna said in a hushed, almost reverent tone. "Custodian is waiting for us."

Chapter 27

T he sound of running water, and the splash and patter of crystal fountains replaced what once had been a heavy, dry silence. There was a difference in the air. EDDIE had felt it as soon as they made it to the surface. It was as if something stale had been cleared away, and a window had been opened to let breezes into a room that had been closed up for a long time.

Soft, pale things were flitting around the overgrown gardens, nipping dead branches into small twigs, and even smaller twigs and catching them before they hit the ground. They swooped the twigs away through bubbles of shadow that were there for a moment before they popped. Gone before EDDIE could make out what they were.

A butterfly, at least that's what he thought it was, flitted in and landed for a moment or two right between EDDIE's micro-dot-camera eyes. It opened its iridescent wings, then closed them, and waggled its antennae. It seemed in no hurry at all to be anywhere other than where it was. EDDIE fancied he could feel the tickle of its feet. After a time, it gave a little flap and lifted into the air, drifting off to be lost in the warm shade of the trees.

They found Custodian at the confluence of four brooks: arteries of pulsating deep green energy. He was a fountain: full and robust and tall, from which gemstones fell, like green rain. They fell, bounced, and rolled, coming together with other droplets to form small pools. After a moment or two, the pools flowed together, forming a green trickle that wandered its way back into the heart of the garden where Custodian stood. EDDIE remembered that the place had once seemed so dead. It was now fully alive.

"Welcome again EDDIE," Custodian said, his voice was now large and cool as a pool of deep water on a hot day. "As is plain, we are relieved, and our thanks are given to you. We now call you *friend.*"

EDDIE felt Vosna glow with approval, but he was unable to look away from Custodian.

"You have done much, little one," said Custodian. "But there is much still to do."

"I know," EDDIE agreed. Somewhere deep inside he knew the importance of Custodian's words.

"We can help," Custodian told him, "But only from a distance, only in part, only so much."

"Any help I can get, is better than no help at all. I am not going to say no," EDDIE admitted to himself.

From somewhere Custodian produced a small purple cube. It rotated, tumbling on its axis, end over end, a centimeter or two above the flat surface of Custodian's extruded tendril.

"EDDIE, this is Artifact."

EDDIE felt an intense moment of anticipation as Custodian reached toward his chest.

Custodian's tendril melted into nothing. It dissipated through EDDIE's metal skin, evaporating within. EDDIE sensed a bubble of energy swelling inside him. It was spreading everywhere, coating his valves and his central processor. Whatever Artifact was it had touched EDDIE right to his core. He could feel it sitting there, in the middle of his chest, spinning slowly.

EDDIE didn't fully understand what was happening, but he wasn't afraid. He knew that Custodian meant him no harm. He had called EDDIE a friend, and when you gave a friend a gift it was always something good. EDDIE realised that Artifact was something that Custodian wanted EDDIE to have. EDDIE didn't know what Artifact did, but he knew that it was something important.

Of all the places that Artifact had touched, it had not come near EDDIE's neural cortex. EDDIE sensed that Artifact wanted to help, but it didn't want EDDIE to be something EDDIE wasn't.

"I am still me," EDDIE announced with total conviction, and he knew it was true.

"Artifact is enabled," Custodian said, his deep crystal voice ringing clear as a bell through the grove.

"You will decide what it can do. It will be something that it agrees with, but first you must come to trust it, as it also trusts you." Custodian said. "Whatever it is, you must be mutual. You are already mutual. In agreement. Together. It is together ... equal ... in partnership that you will grow."

It didn't make sense to EDDIE. It wasn't something he understood right now, but he knew, eventually, he'd get it. To *infer* things, you needed more data than he had right now. As time went on, he was sure he'd figure it out.

Artifact stirred in EDDIE's chest. For a moment he was back in the pump room, standing near the open hatchway. Beside him floated the body of Engineer, First Class. What purpose did Artifact have bringing it to mind now? EDDIE knew it was important, but he didn't know why. EDDIE wondered what he had missed? He felt Artifact reassure him; whatever it was EDDIE was supposed to remember would come to him.

"Little robot," Custodian said. "You are only as small as you think you are. We know that you will do great things." This left EDDIE feeling as if his future mattered, that he could do what he needed to. Whatever that was.

In that instant EDDIE no longer felt limited by his size. If Custodian said it, he knew, he could achieve anything.

"Still," Custodian shimmered and pulsed. "Though we are optimistic, there are ... problems ... riddles ... mysteries ... to answer, to solve, to unravel."

EDDIE hovered quietly, hardly daring to move. Custodian held every atom of his attention.

"You are part of this now," Custodian told him. "You are part of us."

EDDIE wondered what that meant, but he dared not ask. Was there an affinity he wasn't aware of? Had this place claimed a part of him? It was not home, and it never would be, but it had become somewhere very important to him.

He looked at Vosna. This was now a place of memories, and of adventure, and friendship found.

Almost as an afterthought Custodian turned and spoke to Vosna. "EDDIE has done much with your assistance. There is much still to be done and we must continue to rely on your service."

Vosna bobbed but kept her silence.

"Are you open to all that lies ahead?" Custodian rippled. "What are your true capabilities?"

Vosna flushed hot orange.

"We are pleased with you, one who is Vosna."

Vosna seemed to be trembling, either in fear or anticipation, or pride. It was hard for EDDIE to tell.

"We acknowledge that First Engineer is gone," Custodian said. "We lose what matters ... is important ... close. It is the way of things. It is the process. Cold ... harsh ... uncaring it might seem. It is necessary for us to ... continue."

There was an awkwardness about Vosna's silence. EDDIE sense that something important was about to happen.

"What is broken needs to be repaired ... replaced ... rebuilt," Custodian told her. "This is something only a First Engineer is equipped to oversee."

Vosna was very, very still.

"Are you prepared?"

Vosna made a small noise, giving her ascent. EDDIE could tell she was nervous. She had no idea what was going to happen. What was Custodian about to do?

"Then ... *be* ... First Engineer Vosna," Custodian said, opening her mind to receive the knowledge she had been missing. "So it is and so you are."

Chapter 28

"Come," said Custodian, turning now to EDDIE. "Come." The word was hardly more than a hint of a whisper in the voice emulator. "We will once again reveal to you Archive. There you will find your means of return."

Archive seemed bigger than EDDIE remembered: Objects both unknown and familiar were now all supported by strong, steady shafts of phosphorescent green.

"Oh, that is beautiful," Vosna said in the deepest appreciation as she took in the wonderful, new and different things, machines most extraordinary.

"There is time to satisfy your hunger to know, First Engineer Vosna," Custodian said. "Time enough for you to discover and continue to discover the knowledge you have just been given. But now it is time for you to assist our friend, EDDIE."

Vosna gave her version of a nod and turned to EDDIE. "How did you come to be here?"

"Well," EDDIE said, "One moment I was on Crafty's desk as he tuned in the old radio set, hoping to send the Muk'Vuh back where it came from, and the next I was here, lying on the grass, with the Muk'Vuh sitting on my head."

"Most strange. That science is unfamiliar." She wiggled in thought. "Some of that signal might yet remain. Once we find the signal we can focus and amplify the connection."

EDDIE allowed himself to feel hopeful. The concept of home filled him with a warm glow.

"You see," Vosna explained, "The Translocation I know happens between places that … how to describe it… *know* each other, places that are familiar with each other, places that are in some way the same."

EDDIE wasn't sure how that applied. Was the grass enough to make a connection? There had been no grass on Crafty's workbench, and Earth was certainly different to Vosna's world. The workbench was made of wood, but there were no trees on the hill where he had first arrived.

"Places need not have started out the same," Vosna tried to explain. "It will work if they have been made the same."

EDDIE glanced at Custodian, a column of liquid energy, rising and falling.

Does our being in a place change that place in some way? EDDIE wondered. If we are with someone, do we leave something of ourselves behind? They are changed by us, and we are changed by them. EDDIE wondered if that was the same idea. He had been changed by Vosna being his friend. He knew they would remember their time together, and yes; her world had been different before EDDIE came. It would be different after he went home. She was First Engineer now and EDDIE had helped her to get there.

"We must search Archive for an untuned translocator," Vosna told him.

EDDIE had no idea how any of this would work, because the technology was so unfamiliar to him. He knew one thing. He trusted Vosna. They had only been friends for a short time, and yet she had proved her worth. He knew he could rely on her.

"We have learned much together, friend EDDIE," Vosna said. "But we have much yet to learn."

She laughed in delight. "We should grow, all the time in what we know. That's what life is for after all. Growing and learning."

"She is right," EDDIE knew.

She meandered her way down the ranks of Archive. EDDIE followed. If he knew what each item did, he might have seen there was order to the arrangement. Thing went with thing; like with like. Every now and again he recognised that if you placed items together, they would fit, and make a whole, and function in some designed way. It was much like the warehouse, but here what was stored was old, and long forgotten.

They came to a halt at the end of a long row of gadgets that had all started to look the same. "Vosna," EDDIE asked. "Why don't we just ask Archive for what we want? I mean, doesn't it have a search function?"

"Oh, EDDIE, you are such a genius," Vosna glowed at him. "But where would the fun be in that? Surely you have places like this where you are from? You can go in and wander around and walk down the lines and lanes of discovery, finding designs from long ago, learning stuff you didn't know? What a wonderful way to spend time?"

EDDIE must have transmitted his impatience.

Vosna sighed. "Oh, perhaps you are right. You are keen to return to home."

EDDIE felt a sub-link of the voice emulator come alive, as Vosna communicated with Archive. He heard the distinct sounds of a data handshake, the crackles and screeches, of tones matching and becoming modular before settling into their song of connection.

It wasn't long before what they wanted appeared on several nearby platforms. *"Of course,"* EDDIE groaned, *"it would come in a flat pack."* Vosna set about taking the items and putting them onto a transport platform she had retrieved from somewhere that EDDIE hadn't seen. She stacked what they needed higher than EDDIE thought sensible, but Vosna seemed confident it wasn't all about to slide off onto the ground.

"Now, friend EDDIE, we need to find your node."

"What's a node?"

"That place of signal parity," Vosna explained. "It will be near where you came through."

EDDIE pointed to the hills east of the city. "Up there," he said.

Vosna looked to Custodian with some uncertainty. "How can I do this?" She asked.

Custodian reached out a tendril, and Vosna was enveloped by the shimmering green of his touch. It faded slowly until she was her amber self again.

"You are no longer tethered, First Engineer." Custodian told her. "There is no restriction. Now complete it as you see fit."

Vosna stifled her whoop. She was free.

"Come, friend EDDIE, let's get you home."

Chapter 29

E DDIE felt a pang of regret as they made their way out of the city, followed by the transport platform laden with parts, big and small and stuff in boxes yet to be unpacked.

"Will I be back?" EDDIE wondered. *"If all this works out, do I get to come back?"* Again, he felt there was a sense he was leaving things unfinished.

"I'd like to meet with Custodian again," EDDIE said when they came to a stop. "Some time."

Standing on the hillside, not far from that spot where he had first appeared, it occurred to EDDIE he had come full circle.

"What makes you think you won't, friend EDDIE?" Vosna asked.

"Oh, I don't know really."

"I can reassure you like this," Vosna told him, indicating the translocator that she was starting to assemble. "Once this translocator is installed, once it has made the connection, when it is fully linked place to place, now to now, it will always be open and ready and listening. You see, it will know its frequency, and there will be only one that it can know, no other."

"Vosna," EDDIE asked following through with a sudden hunch. "Can you have a translocator linked to multiple places at once?"

Vosna considered this for a time. "That friend EDDIE I am unable to answer. Why would it be necessary?"

"I was thinking about our friends, the Muk'Vuh."

"Ah," Vosna bobbed. "Yes, I see. Our problem comes in not knowing the location of their home. We would not be able to establish the link."

"We don't know their home, but they do."

Vosna gave EDDIE an appreciative look. "I enjoy the way you think, friend EDDIE. It makes sense that this is something we should investigate. But it is for a future time. Now we must focus on you and your return to where you belong."

"Will the harness come with me? Will it work when I get home?"

Vosna laughed. "Unless you come from another universe. The same laws apply here as they do where you are from. Of this I am certain."

"And if this doesn't work?" EDDIE asked, indicating the translocator.

Vosna jiggled. "Then we invent something that will! We will come up with something not yet crafted, something new. Remember friend EDDIE, the way of the Engineer? It's my way now, and I suspect it might also be yours. I think this is something we share. Yes?"

Vosna continued to assemble the translocator as she talked. A hexagon was taking slow shape on the ground. EDDIE remarked at the difference. This was not at all like the one he had stepped onto when he needed a quick return from the pump room.

"You are right friend EDDIE; Archive has given us a translocator of different design. I have not seen this design before, but in many ways, it is the same, in the important things it is the same, it will work the same, and do the same, and be the same when it is complete."

Vosna set the final piece into place. She checked to see if everything was connected, and bobbed back, surveying her handiwork. "Yes, we are almost done," she said. "And we are positioned right on the node. This is something I can sense. There is energy here. We will have plenty of power, and plenty of signal."

She waved a tendril hand over the side of the device. "Please, friend EDDIE, step close, it needs your proximity so it can calibrate."

The hexagon glowed white, amber, yellow, green, then settled into a shade of deep sky blue. "Ahhh, already it has attuned itself to you, EDDIE. Your home signal gives it that colour, you give it that colour." She considered this for a moment. "Your world must be very beautiful."

"I wish you could come with me," EDDIE said.

"I am not tethered," Vosna said gently. "This is true. I could come. But I am needed here."

"Yes," EDDIE said, trying to keep the sadness out of his voice. "You are."

"And yet," Vosna mused, "We are now linked."

"Linked?"

"Yes, can you not feel it?"

There was something different down in EDDIE's chest. There was the lightness of Artifact, with its glow suffusing all that he was, and keeping everything focused.

"I know I am different than before," EDDIE confessed.

"I see you friend EDDIE. You are a shimmer in the pattern now."

EDDIE looked at Vosna. There was a solidity to her, a deeper sense of her presence that was new. He didn't know what the pattern was, but he was aware of a strong impression of place, and of the moment. Where he was standing was more real, it seemed. He knew that it was one of those things he would understand as time went on.

"Custodian has enabled the way," Vosna observed, "Be of good cheer friend EDDIE, Custodian has given us the means to communicate. I remain here, but we are connected because we are friends."

"We are? He has?"

"Yes, we are. And yes, he has. Trust me, friend EDDIE, you will see."

EDDIE felt deeply reassured.

EDDIE felt the closeness of home for the first time. He felt it tugging at him, drawing him toward the translocator.

"It doesn't feel real," EDDIE thought, though he knew it was.

"It's time friend EDDIE. The translocator will remain on and locked, no one can change the signal at this end now it has been set. I cannot vouch for the signal the other end."

EDDIE was certain Crafty would have left the radio set on and receiving; like leaving a light on in a window just in case. He gave the joystick a little nudge and floated into the energy field.

"See you soon, friend EDDIE."

The football sized amber teardrop that was Vosna faded to black.

Chapter 30

At first EDDIE felt nothing other than an itch deep inside his chest between his valves.

Suddenly his whole being flashed an intense blue, as bright as summer lightning that faded quickly to silver moonlight, with a persistent darkness around the edges. There was an avalanche of sound, but that faded quickly.

He felt his head rattle as if it wasn't quite where it should be, and he had a moment of panic. He had no sense of place, *here* was still unresolved: for the moment there was nothing for him to latch onto. "Where am I?" EDDIE asked no one in particular.

Had he heard a screen door bang? It might have been that which silenced the cricket he realised had been singing without much enthusiasm underneath a bright square of glass that surely was a window. Slowly EDDIE became aware that he was sprawled on his left side, unable to move. His legs felt funny. Were they broken? It felt like they were partly detached.

Almost unconsciously he reached out, "Vosna?"

Her voice came from a distance but not as far away as he had expected. "I am here EDDIE," she said happily. "I told you I would be. I told you it would work."

"Vosna, where am I?"

"You haven't figured that out?" Vosna sighed. "Silly little ro-bot. If all is well, then you are home."

"Thank you Vosna," EDDIE whispered across the voice emu-lator.

"You are welcome, friend EDDIE."

Suddenly the shed door flew open and light burst all around him. EDDIE's micro-dot-cameras blinked to adjust. They were no longer glowing green but were now the deepest blue.

"EDDIE? EDDIE!! EDDIE! It is you! It is you!"

I know that voice. "Crafty?"

Crafty, tousle-haired, and sleepy, now filled EDDIE's vision. He had been in such a hurry to get to the shed he had forgotten to put on his glasses, and he was squinting to make out what was in front of him. "EDDIE! Oh. Wow. It really is you."

"I certainly hope so."

EDDIE heard Kepler's questioning growl at the door and heard his wagging black and white tail thumping against the wall.

Without ceremony, or invitation Helix, the cat vaulted onto the bench, and gave EDDIE a flurry of sandpaper licks, and re-peatedly rubbed and her chin against him, purring heavily. Mrs McKenzie eventually reasserted her control and surveyed the scene. She said in what she hoped was a stern voice: "Where have you been, you *naughty* little robot, we have all been wor-ried sick. I've had chronic fur balls since you were whisked away to goodness knows where." She did the only thing she could, she headbutted EDDIE firmly but affectionately. "Don't *ever* do that to us again!"

"What have you done to yourself?!" Crafty cried in alarm. He was peering at EDDIE's broken legs, and at all the scrapes and dents. "You are a total, absolute, complete and utter *mess*!"

"Ah, I'm glad you noticed." EDDIE sighed. "*I might be a mess,*" he said to himself, "*But I'm a happy mess all the same.*"

"Where have you been?" Crafty asked.

"Now, there's a story," EDDIE said. He felt the warmth of a smile flow through his valves. "I have so much to tell you. For the moment though, I am just so happy to be home."

In his mind's eye, far away, but very close, EDDIE felt his friend Vosna smile and nod.

On impulse Crafty scooped EDDIE up from the bench and folded him in a big, relieved, and happy hug.

"Welcome home, EDDIE, welcome home."

EDDIE will return to continue his adventures

in

EDDIE
and the
Haunted Mansion

Acknowledgments

EDDIE first came to visit me several years ago, while I was lying sick in bed with bronchitis.

The image of a little robot popped into my head.

"Who are you?" I asked.

"My name is EDDIE," he told me.

"Hello, EDDIE," I said.

He must have liked the place because he hung around. He's a patient little guy because it was ages before I paid enough attention to him to sit down and write his story.

Along the way, a lot of people helped.

My wonderful wife Lyndal took the early draft and put it to the red pen, suggesting lots of changes, telling me what worked and what didn't, and letting me know when I slipped, yet again, into passive voice. I am grateful to her for her help in making this a better story. She revealed hidden talents as Editor Supreme. My son Jared also read some of the early manuscript and suggested changes.

I want to extend a huge thank you to my beta readers Peter J. Crooke and Richard Morse. They both helped in different ways. Thanks guys.

An early draft of EDDIE was entered into the *Publishable* competition run by the Queensland Writers Centre from which I received valuable feedback and encouragement.

The cover design and art came up so much better than I could ever have dreamed, and I have my friends Laura and Roger Burgin to thank for bringing my characters to life in full colour. I am indebted to Stephanie McBean for the amazing concept sketches she did for EDDIE at the very beginning of the project. It was Stephanie's sketch that I sent through to Laura and Roger and said, "This is EDDIE!"

They say writing a book is a journey, and when I look back to where my writing journey began, long before EDDIE came to stay, I want to say a huge thank you to my friend and fellow writer Kate Walker, who taught me the basics and had faith in my writing.

The bio bit

C.C. Parfoot was born in the icy cold bitter howling winds of New Zealand and came to the egg frying heat of Australia when he was eleven. He's older now and has lots of grey hair and makes his home in Brisbane with his wife, and three sons.

When he's not writing C.C. Parfoot enjoys reading, playing his ukulele, singing, and trying not to kill the house plants. One orchid has died, but he promises the rest are OK.

He spends way too much time watching You Tube and can't seem to convince his family to play Scrabble with him.

Disclaimer

No cats, dogs or robots were permanently harmed in the writing of this book. The author cannot vouch for the mental or digestive health of the Muk'Vuh.